TOTALLY CONFIDENTIAL

TOTALLY CONFIDENTIAL

Sally Warner

HarperCollins*Publishers*

Library of Congress Cataloging-in-Publication Data
Warner, Sally.
    Totally confidential / Sally Warner.
       p.   cm.
    Summary: After dispensing good advice to her clients, professional listener Quinney finds herself in need of
advice for dealing with her weird family and changing relationships with her best friends.
    ISBN 0-06-028261-4. — ISBN 0-06-028262-2 (lib. bdg.)
    [1. Family life—Fiction.   2. Best friends—Fiction.   3. Friendship—Fiction.]   I. Title.
PZ7.W24644To   2000   99-36101
[Fic]—dc21   CIP
                                                                                                   AC

Typography by Matt Adamec   1 2 3 4 5 6 7 8 9 10   ❖   First Edition

For Sally Johnson (SallyOne),
my first—and best—Lake Luzerne friend,
from SallyToo!

Contents

Chapter One

Listening

"So, should I get a divorce, or what?" the round-faced woman asked Mary McQuinn Todd across the gleaming table. They were sitting in the rear room of the tiny Lake Geneva Public Library in upstate New York, surrounded by reference books. It was a hot and sticky summer afternoon, but the thick stone walls of the old building made it feel cool inside. Quinney scheduled all her listening appointments to start fifteen minutes before the library closed, which made it easier to stop each session promptly when the time was up.

Quinney stared at the woman in shock, her green eyes unblinking. She tried to look calm. She thought hard as she twiddled a strand of her reddish hair—which she always insisted was brown. "You do know I'm only twelve, don't you, Mrs. Ryder?" she asked.

"Ms.," the woman corrected Quinney.

"Oh, sorry," Quinney said, surprised. Not many women in Lake Geneva called themselves *Ms.*

1

"So you're twelve. What's your point?" the big woman asked sharply, shifting in her creaking chair. "You do give advice, don't you? You took my dollar fast enough."

Quinney watched Ms. Ryder's violet T-shirt rise and fall with the woman's indignant breaths. "Well, my ad says professional *listener*," she finally pointed out.

"Same thing," Ms. Ryder snapped.

"Giving advice would depend on the question," Quinney said. "I mean, on how easy the question was."

"Your ad just said 'No medical advice given,' period. This isn't medical, it's personal."

"It sure is," Quinney said, thinking of the woman's long, involved story.

Quinney Todd was famous among her friends and family for her calm demeanor and common sense. But she was *too* calm and *too* sensible, she sometimes felt.

For example, why was *she* always the one who had to patch things up when a squabble broke out between Brynn and Marguerite, her two best friends? And why did her parents count on *her* to handle disputes between her two little brothers and their invisible friend, Monty?

Still, that's the way things were—she was always the

peacemaker. And so I might as well make it pay, she had thought.

Pay, as in money.

So Quinney decided to go into the listening business for the summer.

The idea had come to her a month earlier when one morning at breakfast her dad said, "Hey, listen to this!" and started to read aloud from the newspaper. Some lady who'd just gotten married had written in to an advice column, complaining that her new husband didn't like it when her three big hound dogs slept on the bed.

"People are just amazing," Quinney's mother said, laughing and shaking her head.

Quinney chewed on an English muffin while she listened to her father read the new bride's letter, and she thought, What advice would *I* give her?

"I think she should take her husband to the pound," Teddy declared, pink with rage. Teddy was five years old and a fierce animal lover.

"Yeah," Mack chimed in, loyal to his twin. Both boys then shoveled cereal into their mouths, invigorated by their anger.

"What about you, Quinney?" her father had asked. "What do you think the woman should do?"

Quinney swallowed her bite of muffin and wiped

her mouth with a napkin. "I think she should make the dogs sleep in the hall. And she should shut the bedroom door and apologize to her husband," she finally said.

"*Boo,*" Teddy muttered. "I never say I'm sorry!" Mack gazed at him in admiration.

"We know, Teddy-bear," Mr. Todd said, laughing. "But the columnist said exactly the same thing that Quinney did."

"She *did*?" Quinney and Teddy said together.

Quinney took a sip of orange juice and waited for things to quiet down. "Dad," she asked, after the twins had tumbled out of the kitchen and into the backyard, "do people really get paid for answering questions like that?"

"Sure—psychologists do," her father said. "They make a fortune, too." He sighed and took off his glasses, polishing the butter-smudged lenses absentmindedly on an edge of the red-and-white plaid tablecloth. Norman Todd taught high school math, and he did *not* make a fortune.

"Huh," Quinney said thoughtfully.

"They don't even need to answer any questions, not really," Mr. Todd said, shaking his head. "Sometimes I think that all people really want is for someone just to *listen* for a change."

"Huh," Quinney had repeated, her green eyes shining.

It was so obvious, really!

In fact, Quinney couldn't believe she hadn't thought of it before. She would put an ad in the local *Save-a-Cent*. Readers' ads were free, after all; reply boxes were even provided free of charge. The weekly publication made its money from business advertising.

Nearly everyone in the three-town rural area of Lake Geneva, Marathon, and Rocky Creek read *Save-a-Cent*. Her ad had run the following week, appearing between *Lose Weight Fast!* and *For Sale: Double-Wide Trailer*:

PROFESSIONAL LISTENER
Will listen to what you have to say. $1 for 15 minutes. No medical advice given. Totally confidential! Write c/o Box 112, Save-a-Cent, 112 Main Street, Lake Geneva, New York

Just listening. It sounded so easy.

But now, two weeks into it, Quinney's summer job was proving to be more challenging than she'd expected when she'd first mailed in her ad. Because even though people *said* that all they wanted was someone to listen to them, they really wanted more.

They wanted answers.

Quinney kind of wished she could tell her dad what she'd discovered, but her summer job was a secret. She knew that her parents would have tried to talk her out of doing something so crazy if they'd known about it in advance.

Or worse, they'd have teased her. Two against one. And Quinney *hated* being teased.

Even Brynn and Marguerite didn't know about Quinney's secret summer job. But Quinney couldn't think about them just now. She had work to do.

Technically, Quinney thought, staring across the library table at the violet expanse of Ms. Ryder, she had already almost earned her dollar. She had spent eleven of the fifteen minutes listening to the woman's marital problems, she'd allowed one minute to explain that marriage wasn't really her specialty, and now it was time to wrap things up. "Have you two seen a marriage counselor yet?" she asked.

"Can't afford one. Anyway, Spike wouldn't go even if we had the money. And if we *had* the money, I probably wouldn't be sitting here, complaining—we'd be taking a vacation. We'd be at Disney World, having a ball! Hah. No mouse ears for me in *this* lifetime. I can't get him to go any farther than Peters Falls," she claimed, naming the nearest big town. "He says he doesn't want to put any extra wear and tear on the car. Sometimes I think he loves that Mustang more than he loves me."

As usual, Quinney stuck to the main point, ignoring mouse ears and Mustangs. Sticking to the point was one of her specialties. "And you've been married how long? Sixteen years?"

"Right. No kids."

Thank goodness, Quinney thought. She would have felt sorry for any kids this large, grouchy woman and her apparently stubborn, cautious husband might have had. As if kids didn't have enough problems without difficult parents, she thought. Aloud, she asked, "Did you ever want children? Or did Mr. Ryder?"

"Nope," Ms. Ryder said, her voice firm.

"But you wanted each other."

"Yep," Ms. Ryder said, sounding a little doubtful this time.

"Why?" Quinney asked.

"I told you—"

"Excuse me, but you told me what's *wrong* with your husband, not what you like about him," Quinney said, lowering her voice and looking around the library nervously. She hoped that neither Brynn nor Marguerite would walk in on this hot July day. If they did, she would have some explaining to do!

Not to mention how awful it would be if Cree Scovall found out. Not that he was a friend, exactly. Not that he knew she existed, exactly. No such luck.

"Hmmph," Ms. Ryder said, not pleased at this line of questioning. "Well," she finally said, sounding reluctant, "Spikey was funny—he made me laugh. He still *can*, when he gets off his duff."

Spikey! Quinney thought, stifling a giggle. She pictured a small barking terrier, wiry fur sticking up. Ms. Ryder seemed more like a big English sheepdog. "Anything else you like about him?" she asked. She nibbled on the end of her black felt-tip pen as she listened.

"He's a good dancer," Ms. Ryder admitted, swaying a little. "Which is part of the problem," she added, heating up again. "Like I told you, he never wants to go anywhere, now. He always says, 'Been there, done that.' That's Spikey's motto, practically. His *mantra*," she added, leaning forward. Her white hands stopped waving around to imaginary dance music and gripped the golden oak table like a hungry starfish.

"I'm sorry to interrupt you," a voice said, "but the library is closing."

I love you, Mrs. Arbuckle, Quinney thought. The librarian was definitely an old-fashioned Mrs., complete with half glasses and gray hair pulled back into a tidy bun. She was new in town, and so she didn't know Quinney. She never seemed to show any curiosity about the listening appointments, though, and she always kicked out Quinney and her customer at exactly the right time. In fact, Quinney counted on Mrs. Arbuckle's punctuality.

It was all part of the plan.

She waited politely for Mrs. Arbuckle to walk away, and then she turned to Ms. Ryder, cleared her throat, and said, "This will have to conclude our first meeting, I'm afraid. My advice is for you to think of five things you still like about Mr. Ryder. About—um—Spike," she clarified, blushing a little. "If you want to make another appointment, write me in care of the *Save-a-Cent* box number, and I'll call you to set up a time. Oh, and it would be helpful if you'd bring the list with you the next time we meet. If we meet again."

"Why do I have to write you? Can't you just give me your phone number?" Ms. Ryder asked, irritated.

"Uh-uh, sorry," Quinney said firmly, shaking her head. What an idea! she thought.

Quinney swatted at a cartoonlike cloud of gnats swirling above her head as she walked the few blocks home from the library. She retucked her spotless white T-shirt into pleated denim shorts and gazed down in dismay at her skinny legs. My knees look *huge*, she thought.

Although no one was there to see it, Quinney made

a face. Ms. Ryder, calling *her* house! She could just picture it—and the embarrassing questions that would follow.

But it wasn't simply that she wanted to keep her job a secret, Quinney admitted to herself as she kicked at a soggy branch that had blown down during the last summer thunderstorm. No. No *way* was she going to let important business calls come into her family's crazy house! She had to keep the two things away from each other.

The orderly life in her head, and the jumbled life with her family.

Separate.

That was the great thing about having a box at *Save-a-Cent*—it kept things separate. And maybe that was even why she liked her secret summer job so much, in spite of the difficulties it posed. It allowed her to deal with people one-on-one for a change, instead of the crowds—Teddy and Mack, her mom and dad, Brynnie and Marguerite—she was generally stuck with.

Quinney waved at Mr. Sansom, their neighbor. He was just backing his old Toyota out of his driveway. Now there was a normal guy, she thought, fiddling with the latch to the front gate. And the Sansoms were a normal family, too. Not like hers; not at all.

Oh, the Todds *looked* normal from the outside,

Quinney knew. Their house did, anyway. It was set back from the quiet road that ran past the lake. It was two stories high and painted white with blue-gray shutters and doors and was surrounded by a neatly trimmed lawn.

Her family consisted of the normal assortment of parents and children, Quinney thought—one dad, one mom, and three kids. Quinney did not count the twins' invisible friend, Monty, of course.

But once a person shut the front door, normal went out the window.

Quinney shoved the gate closed. It was swollen from all the rain they'd been having that summer. It had rained so much that there was moss on the sidewalks. Her dad's car was parked in the driveway, which meant he was home from work.

Norman Todd taught high school in nearby Rocky Creek during the school year, and he worked at the Sears in Peters Falls during the summer, selling computer equipment. Many people in the area had more than one job, since the pay for any single job was usually so low; it was called "Making an Adirondack Living."

Quinney imagined that all her dad's students and department store customers probably thought he was as ordinary as could be. But when he got home,

Norman Todd let his real personality out of its suit-and-tie disguise.

He became a Mark Twain–style riverboat captain, complete with navy blue cap. "Well, we *do* live next to a river," he often pointed out. "It's not my fault it's the Hudson and not the Mississippi!" That seemed to be his only regret in life. At least the Hudson River was still protected and unspoiled in this southernmost part of the Adirondack State Park.

Quinney's father loved the writings of Mark Twain and collected anything about him he could find. He even had a huge mahogany steering wheel from an old paddleboat mounted on the living room wall. That was his prize, unearthed in a cluttered old store during a family vacation trip to Hannibal, Missouri—Mark Twain's hometown. They had driven all the way back to New York with the wheel strapped to the roof of their car.

People had *honked* at them. Quinney had just about died.

She was probably the only kid in her school who had been dragged to Missouri for vacation, she thought, slamming the door. *She'd* probably never get to Disney World, either.

And her dad did other weird things, too—like

working on hopeless projects in the basement and quoting Aesop's fables at breakfast.

Norman Todd was not like any of her friends' fathers—the ones who were around, anyway.

Her mother was unusual, too, Quinney thought, frowning. Marnie Todd was an artist, but she didn't act the way Quinney thought an artist should act. An artist should be carefree, whimsical, a free spirit.

Oh, she dressed the part, usually wearing long, gauzy skirts and sandals—at least in the summer. Winters, she wore leggings under the skirts, and a parka. She looked weird enough for an artist, Quinney conceded.

But she was no free spirit. She stuck to her working schedule like Super Glue. Her artwork was all she could think about, practically—well, that, and her husband.

And that was the most unnormal thing of all: Quinney's dad and mom were still crazy about each other after seventeen years of marriage. They're like teenagers in love, Quinney thought, scowling. It was embarrassing, the way they acted when they were together. Flirting, holding hands.

In fact, sometimes Quinney thought that her parents were *too* crazy about each other.

Whenever the family went to the movies, her parents *had* to sit next to each other. Quinney always ended up sitting between the twins so they wouldn't poke each other and giggle. Her parents fed each other bites of food in restaurants while Quinney refereed Teddy and Mack.

Quinney's mom even sat on her husband's lap sometimes. Well, not at the movies or in restaurants, thank goodness—just on the old striped sofa at home. But *still.*

A mom and dad should love each other, sure, Quinney thought, getting a carton of orange juice out of the refrigerator, but not like girlfriend and boyfriend. That was kind of disgusting.

It was as though her parents were complete all by themselves, she thought—just the two of them. They didn't seem to need anyone else. Quinney imagined that they might even have been surprised when she had been born. She pictured them standing with their arms around each other, blinking in astonishment as they peered into her crib. . . .

What have we done? they probably asked each other.

Quinney took a sip of the cool juice.

But then seven years later the twins had been born, and Quinney remembered how joyously the boys' births had been awaited. So her mom and dad *must* have wanted kids.

The funny thing was, though, she still felt like an orphan sometimes.

The twins didn't seem to think anything was wrong with their family. But they were still little. Only five years old—what did *they* know?

And they had each other. Like her mom and dad had each other.

And that left Quinney, all alone.

She had her listening business, of course. That was all hers.

Quinney sloshed some water in her empty glass. "Hey, I'm home!" she called out, pushing open the swinging door that led to the front hall. "Where is everybody?"

Chapter Two

Drumbeat

The lake that gave the town of Lake Geneva its name was not where Quinney and her friends liked to gather during the summer. In fact, they usually avoided its one small public beach and the scraggly park that wrapped around it, close as it was to Quinney's house. Too crowded, they all agreed. Not enough privacy.

Which really meant—Quinney admitted to herself—that it was older kids who hung out there, perched like big sullen birds on the scattered picnic tables.

A lot of Quinney's classmates liked to meet up at the town's tennis courts if it wasn't too hot and buggy, but she, Brynnie, and Marguerite preferred the narrow park that the creek ran through, behind the historical society building on Main Street. They had claimed the area for their own that summer—not that anyone else seemed to want it.

The creek, which tunneled under a road near Lake Geneva and then down a gentle slope, fed into the nearby Hudson River. It didn't even have a name as far as Quinney knew. But she loved it.

It was Saturday afternoon, and Quinney, Brynn, and Marguerite were sprawled on the limp grass next to the creek, talking. Brynn's soft voice blended with the sound of rushing water, and Quinney had to listen hard to make out what she was saying.

"I'm just sure my mom won't let me go to any party on Mahoney's Hill," Brynnie stated. "She wouldn't even let me go river rafting on the Sacandaga that time, and that was in broad daylight." Brynn twirled a wispy strand of blond hair around her finger and sighed.

Marguerite shrugged, and turned to Quinney. She lifted her long brown hair away from her neck, then let it fall against her thin, angular face. She tugged at the bottom of her bra, then started picking at her toenail polish. "What about you, Quinney? You want to come to the party?" she asked, an *I-dare-you* in her voice. "Cree Scovall will probably be there," she added, looking sideways at her friend. "Yum, yum." She grinned.

"Cree Scovall is fourteen years old, and he doesn't know—or *care*—about any of us," Quinney said, trying to sound bored. "Why should he?" she added. "He's barely even met anyone in Lake Geneva yet."

17

The Scovall family had moved to Lake Geneva that April. The name Cree was short for Christopher, which his little sister couldn't pronounce, or so the newspaper story went.

He'd earned instant fame when that same little sister had wandered off while the family was unpacking from their move. She had just strayed onto the curving road in front of their new house—and into the path of a logging truck, which was barreling along at twice the posted speed—when Cree spotted her and leaped, knocking them both out of harm's way.

One look at the picture of his scraped-up face in the *Peters Falls Press* and reading the accompanying story of the daring rescue was all it took for Quinney.

But how on earth did Marguerite *know?* Quinney had never breathed a word about her crush, because Marguerite teased *and* she could never keep a secret.

Which was why Quinney hadn't told her about the listening business, either. And she knew she couldn't tell Brynn, because Brynn was kind of scared of Marguerite. She might blurt something out in a moment of panic.

"Anyway," Quinney continued, ignoring Marguerite's crack about Cree, "I have to baby-sit the twins tonight. My mom and dad are going out. *Again,*" she added, disapprovingly. She flopped over onto her stomach and picked up a twig. She tried to coax a beetle onto it. The beetle waggled its feelers at the twig, then turned around and trundled off in the opposite direction.

"Carrottop," Brynnie said, tickling the back of Quinney's neck with a blade of grass.

"It's brown," Quinney said lazily, and Marguerite laughed. Quinney flung herself onto her back again.

"Where do your parents go all the time?" Brynn asked, tossing the grass away. Her voice was full of wonder. "I mean, what is there to do around here, anyway?"

Quinney clamped her hands over her eyes, instantly erasing the canopy of maple leaves above her. "I don't know," she said wearily. "They go out for romantic candlelight dinners, or they go bowling, or they drive to Peters Falls and snuggle at the movies. They *date*. I just have to live with it."

"Well, that's plain weird," Marguerite said flatly. "My parents would never go out on a date. Not together, anyway. But forget about your parents. Who cares what parents do? I'm talking about *us*, about our lives! And everyone's going to be there tonight, up on the hill. Some of the guys are even bringing motor-bikes."

"But you're talking about high school kids," Quinney objected. "It's probably only the really crazy ones who'll show up. And riding around those steep trails at night! Something bad happens on that hill every single year, Marguerite. Remember that guy who was in a coma for a week last summer? And that kid who was lying out there all night with his leg broken in three places? Even with a full moon, it's nuts."

"And anyway," Brynn pointed out, looking worried, "the only girls there will be those guys' girlfriends. *Teenagers*. How'd you hear about this party anyway, Marguerite?"

"Some kids were talking. I just heard, that's all," Marguerite said vaguely, stretching her thin tanned arms out straight. Then she clasped them behind her head.

Just so we can see how big her boobs have gotten, Quinney thought, exchanging a secret amused glance with Brynn.

Brynn looked away, hiding a grin. "I'll bet you heard about it at the bowling alley," she said to Marguerite. Marguerite's mom worked at Bowl-A-Lot's snack bar on weekends. Marguerite often helped out.

"But how would you even get to the party?" Quinney asked, curious.

Marguerite shrugged her narrow brown shoulders once again and adjusted a turquoise bra strap. "I'll walk—it can't be more than a mile. And I'm sure I'll be able to get a ride home, after," she added, flipping her hair back.

"What will you tell your mom and dad?" Quinney asked.

"That I'm staying with *you* tonight," Marguerite said, smiling some more, as if this were the best part of her plan. But there was a challenge in her smile. "I'll tell them I'm helping you baby-sit the famous Teddy and Mack. Mom will like that. She thinks you're such a good influence on me, Quinney."

Quinney made a face. Like anyone could influence Marguerite, she thought—a little admiringly.

Marguerite Harper was the one person in town Quinney couldn't really figure out, even though they were friends. And sometimes, when Marguerite was driving her especially nuts, Quinney wondered *why* they were still friends.

Was it habit, because they'd known each other since they were babies, practically?

Was it because Lake Geneva was such a small town that it wouldn't be easy to stop being friends there even if you tried? Although Brynnie, for one, seemed to be trying pull away from Marguerite lately. When she dared.

Still, when things were going well among the three

friends, which was most of the time, Quinney had to admit that she liked hanging out with Marguerite because she was so much fun. Everything seemed a little more exciting, a little more dramatic when Marguerite was around—as though a movie sound track had suddenly started playing. Quinney could almost hear the violins—and there was a drumbeat, always.

There were even times when Quinney wished she could be more like Marguerite. When Marguerite wanted to do something, she did it—she made things happen. She didn't get all hung up on planning or worrying, like Quinney did.

It was strange, Quinney thought, but sometimes, watching her crazy friend was a little like looking in a fun-house mirror. It was as though she were peering at a hidden image of herself, almost.

It's like I can count on her to do the stuff I'd be too scared to do, Quinney thought, remembering the time on Cabbage Night, the night before Halloween, when Marguerite had covered all her neighbors' front doorknobs with Vaseline. She'd even put some on her own doorknob just so people wouldn't get suspicious!

But there were other times when Quinney couldn't help worrying about Marguerite.

Like now, for instance.

"Listen, Marguerite," Brynn was saying, sounding a

little nervous, "you can't just go hang out with a bunch of high school kids. They won't want you. Anyway, if anyone found out that a twelve-year-old was up there partying, too, they'd be in trouble." She tugged a little at her too-tight shorts.

"It'll be dark. I'll be wearing makeup, I'll look older," Marguerite snapped, as if reading from a list. "You guys are so chicken."

"Compared to you, I guess," Quinney agreed calmly as she stood up and brushed strands of grass from her bare legs. Her thoughts were racing, though. What could they say or do to change Marguerite's mind about going to that stupid party? "Anyone would look chicken, next to you," she teased, trying flattery.

Marguerite looked pleased at this. "Well, I've got to do *something* to keep from going nuts in this town. Six more years, and then I'm out of here," she added, making a zooming motion with her hand.

"Lake Geneva isn't so bad," Quinney objected mildly.

A chittering squirrel chased another squirrel overhead, and the three girls watched for a moment. Maple branches quivered, and a few trapped raindrops spattered down on Quinney's head. Marguerite laughed. "Squirrel pee," she said.

"Oh, gross! That's my sign to go," Brynn said. "See

23

you guys here tomorrow?" she added, as Marguerite stood up, too, and straightened her short white shorts, which she'd somehow managed to keep free of dirt smudges and grass stains.

"Yeah, maybe, but later in the day," Marguerite said. "I'll probably want to sleep late. But I should have plenty to tell you—with any luck!"

"Hey, wait a minute, Marguerite—I want to say something," Quinney said after Brynn had pedaled away on her battered red bike.

"About the party?" Marguerite said, grinning. "What, have you changed your mind about going?" The challenging look was on her face again.

"No, I haven't changed my mind—but I really don't think *you* should go. You're going to wreck your reputation."

"I'm going to *make* my reputation, you mean!" Marguerite said, her face looking hard all of a sudden. "God, Quinney. You think you know everything, don't you?"

Quinney frowned. "Hey—be fair. I never said I knew *everything*. I was just trying to—"

"Well, just stop trying so hard," Marguerite interrupted. "Miss Know-It-All! There are some things you *don't* know, Skinny-Quinney. About boys and about parties, for instance. No hard feelings, though," she said, smiling again. "Like I said, I'll have lots to tell you guys tomorrow. So, bye."

"Bye," Quinney murmured, watching Marguerite grow smaller as she crossed the road. "No hard feelings," she echoed, sounding unconvincing—even to herself.

But on Sunday, in spite of Marguerite's tantalizing promises, neither Quinney nor Brynn heard a word from her. Quinney finally got up enough nerve to call the Harpers' house at three in the afternoon, but Mrs. Harper said her daughter was taking a nap. "You teenagers!" she added, laughing. "You kids must have really stayed up late."

That's right, Quinney remembered, blushing, the phone suddenly hot in her hands. Marguerite had lied to her parents about sleeping over at Quinney's house.

"We aren't exactly teenagers yet," Quinney reminded Mrs. Harper, trying to get control of the situation.

"Well, but just about," Mrs. Harper said.

"I guess," Quinney agreed weakly.

Chapter Three

How Will I Know Who You Are?

Tuesday was another hot, sticky day in Lake Geneva. It was Quinney's best day yet as a professional listener; three postcards and one letter were waiting in her box.

Quinney turned over the first postcard while still standing at the counter. As usual, she had waited until the *Save-a-Cent* was empty before going inside. She didn't want anyone discovering her secret.

> Dear Listener,
>   I would like to make an appointment. I have some things to get off my chest, it would be worth a dollar. Please call me at 7238.
>   Sincerely,
>   Sam

Everyone who lived in the area gave only the last four digits of their phone number, since the first three were always the same. It was one of the things Quinney liked about Lake Geneva.

In fact, Lake Geneva was perfect in many ways, Quinney thought—in spite of what Marguerite had said.

Of course, the local leather tanning factory had closed long ago, and the small dairy farms that had once surrounded the town were no longer in operation. And the forest was creeping back almost minute by minute, reclaiming fields that had taken centuries to clear.

Times had definitely changed, and the local people had struggled for years, trying to change too. But things seemed pretty good, Quinney thought. She could barely believe some of the stories her father had told her. He said that only ten or twenty years ago, poor people used to carry their shoes for miles as they walked to the Agway just to keep from wearing out the soles. And then they'd sit down on the steps leading to the store's front door and put their shoes on.

They had their pride, her father said.

Now, most people seemed to have jobs of some sort or other. Sometimes they had to go quite far away.

Perhaps, Quinney thought, she was carrying on her town's brave tradition of making work where she found it.

In Quinney's opinion, Lake Geneva was really the

perfect place for a listening business. Even though she told her few customers to call her Quinney during each one's first appointment, they still didn't know who she was—since Quinney wasn't her real name. Not first nor last. They wouldn't be able to find her in the floppy phone book shared by the three neighboring towns.

Dear Quinney,
  I did what you said, but so far only four good things about Spike. But I want another appointment anyway. The price is right. What about this Thursday, same time. Call me, you have the number.
  Ms. Ryder

Another appointment! Quinney groaned and turned over the third postcard.

Listener:
  I have a problem. You probably can't help. Call me anyway, at 5330.
  C.

Negative attitude, Quinney decided. But she'd give whoever-it-was a call.

Finally she ripped open the small envelope. A birthday

card fell out; the greeting had been carefully crossed out with a green crayon. Inside the card, a message had been printed:

Help, Im lonly. 6163. ps I have the $. Ask for Toby.
    Form Toby

Quinney frowned at this one. A kid, obviously. And a very bad speller. And lonely. What did this Toby person think, that a dollar was going to buy him a friend? But a customer was a customer.

When she got home, Quinney's mom and dad were out in the backyard trying to start the lawn mower. They bobbed up and down over it like colorful wooden toys, her mom in a crayon-yellow T-shirt and a flowered skirt, and her dad wearing bright-red shorts and his beloved navy blue captain's cap.

Mr. Todd gave the mower cord a yank, and the machine sputtered, coughed, and died. Quinney's mother started laughing so hard that she could barely stand. She grabbed her husband's arm for support.

Gee, Quinney thought—they even hung out together when her dad was mowing the lawn. What was the *deal* with them?

Quinney's father saw her and lifted his one free hand in greeting. Quinney waved back.

Teddy and Mack were huddled under the birch tree in last year's tiny yellow swim trunks, playing a game. Monty was probably there, too.

Good. Everyone was outside. It was the perfect time for her to use the phone.

First, she called Ms. Ryder. A man answered, his voice gruff. *Spikey!* Quinney thought.

"Hello, is Ms. Ryder in? This is—this is a friend of hers calling."

"She's never in. She stays busy. Too busy for me anymore, I guess." Spikey sounded sad.

"Oh," Quinney said, startled. That wasn't the way Ms. Ryder had told it. "Well," she said at last, "I'll call later. But please tell her Quinney says it's fine for Thursday."

"Great," Mr. Ryder said, sarcastic. "Something else for her to do. Like she isn't gone enough already."

"Uh, well, good-bye," Quinney said. Hmm, she thought, hanging up the phone.

She telephoned C next, but the line was busy, so she tried Sam. "Hello?" a creaky voice said.

"Hello, is this Sam?"

"Why, yes, it is—Sam Weir," the man said, delighted. "Is this my listener?"

"Yes, but how did you know it was me?" Quinney asked.

"I just figured," he said proudly.

"Well, would you like to make an appointment?" Quinney said. "It's only a dollar, and I'd be happy to hear what you have to say."

"Sure—I have a lot to get off my chest," the man said. "The money's not a problem."

"Okay. Is Wednesday afternoon a good time for you? Tomorrow, at the library?"

"The library? I guess so," the man said. "But how will I know who you are?"

"I'll be sitting at the table over by the dictionary, in the reference room, at four forty-five," Quinney said.

"And I get to talk for the whole fifteen minutes?"

"If you'd like," Quinney said. This one was going to be easy, she thought.

"Oh boy," the man said. "I hardly know where to start!"

After saying good-bye to Sam, Quinney tried C again, but the line was still busy, so she telephoned poor, lonely Toby. A woman answered the phone.

"Hello?"

"Hi, is Toby there?"

"May I ask who this is?"

"It's Quinney. He's expecting the call."

"Oh," the woman said. She sounded a little confused. "Well, he's practicing, but I'll go get him." Quinney could hear piano music in the background as the woman walked away from the phone. A few seconds later, another voice spoke.

"Hello?" it said. Quinney had expected someone about eight or nine years old, even considering the bad spelling, but this kid sounded *young*.

"Is this Toby?" Quinney asked.

"Yes," he whispered. "I wrote you," he added.

"I know, that's why I'm calling. I'm Quinney, the listener. How old are you?"

"Six," he said. "I have a dollar, though."

He was only *six*! Quinney thought she knew all the little kids in town, both real and imaginary, thanks to the twins, but she had never heard them talk about a Toby. "Do you live here in town, Toby?" she asked the boy. "Because I don't have a car, you know."

"I live here in the summer," he said.

"You write very well for a six-year-old," she told him.

"I'm advanced," he informed her. "It's not cursive, though," he said. "And I'm not a very good speller. *Yet*. Will you still talk to me?"

"Do you know where the library is? On Main Street?"

"Yes, but I'm not allowed to cross the street alone.

Can't you just come over to my house?"

"Where do you live?"

"Next to the church with the red door," he said. "It's a blue house with a boat in the driveway. And we have concrete ducks on the lawn. Wearing little straw hats. That are usually wet."

Quinney knew the place—it was only a block from where she lived. "Well," she said, reluctant to change her work pattern, "I guess I could make a house call this one time. We could talk in your front yard."

"Or on the porch," Toby volunteered. "There's even a swing," he added, as if trying to tempt her.

"When is a good time for you, Toby?"

"Now?" he asked.

Now! Well, why not? "It'll be about ten minutes, Toby," she said. "I have one other phone call to make, then I'll walk over there. All right?"

"But hurry, okay?"

The third time Quinney tried, C answered the phone. It was Cree.

Chapter Four

It's Personal

She recognized his voice at once.

Even though she'd never talked to him, she had heard him speak with other kids in the halls at school several times. He usually spoke slowly, as if considering each word. Quinney liked that. "Hello?" he was saying now. "Hello? Is anyone there?"

"Oh, uh, hello?" Quinney said, trying to keep her voice low. She wanted to sound older than she really was. Actually, what she wanted to do was hang up!

"Who is this?"

"Did you respond to my ad, the one in the *Save-a-Cent*?" Quinney asked.

Now Cree was the one to lower his voice. "Yeah, yeah, that was me," he said. He sounded a little embarrassed.

"Well, this is the professional listener calling," Quinney said, sinking down to the floor. She drew her knees up to her chest.

"I guess I want to make an appointment," Cree said. "To talk."

Oh, no! Quinney fought the urge to giggle. She couldn't meet with him in person—he'd find out it was only her!

"Hello?" Cree said, starting to sound a little impatient. "Are you still there?"

"I'm here," Quinney said, scratching a mosquito bite on her knee.

"So how does it work? Where do we meet?" Cree asked.

Quinney thought fast. "We—we talk on the phone. That's how I conduct all my appointments." Telling a little fib was better than dying of embarrassment, she told herself.

"On the phone? Well, I guess that's okay," Cree said. "And it's a dollar?"

"That's right." She probably would have given Cree Scovall *five* dollars just to talk to him for one minute, she thought.

"Do I mail the money before or after we talk?"

"After is all right. You can pay me after," Quinney told him.

"So do we start now?" he asked, impatient again.

"Sure. No, wait," Quinney interrupted herself, suddenly remembering that advanced-but-lonely Toby was waiting for her. "I can't now, I have another appointment."

"Well, when, then?" Cree asked.

"How about tonight, after dinner?"

"Okay, but can you make it later than eight o'clock? My folks are going out then, and I need privacy for this. These appointments are private, aren't they?"

"Oh, yes," she assured him, her voice turning businesslike. "Private and totally confidential. Uh, do you want to tell me your name?"

There was a pause. "Not really," Cree finally said. "I don't think you need to know my name. Just call me C."

"Okay," Quinney said, smiling, "but can you give me some idea of the subject matter so I can be doing some thinking about it? Free of charge, of course."

"I'd rather only have to say it once," Cree told her. "That's going to be bad enough. Let's just say it's *personal*."

"Personal. Okay," Quinney said, her heart seeming to skid and then jump. "Personal. So I'll call you tonight at eight."

"A little after," Cree reminded her.

"Right. Well, thanks for calling." Quinney hung up, then banged her head on the wall next to the phone. *You* called *him*, stupid, she thought. You called him! She banged her head again.

"Monty says to stop that pounding," a little voice scolded. It was Mack. He and Teddy were standing at the door.

"Yeah, he says stop," Teddy confirmed.

"I'm stopping, I'm stopping. And I'm leaving. Tell Mom I'll be back pretty soon, okay? In time to baby-sit you, so they can go out—*again.*"

"Tell her yourself," Mack said.

"Yeah, we're busy playing with Monty."

Toby was sitting right next to the concrete ducks, waiting for her. He had straight black hair that gleamed in the afternoon sunlight. "You're a little bit late," he called out, as she walked toward him.

"How do you know it's me?" she asked. He was bigger than the twins, she thought—stockier, and more neatly dressed than they ever were, too. His little polo shirt was tucked into belted khaki shorts, and he was wearing sandals.

He looked like a miniature businessman on vacation.

"Huh?" he said.

"How do you know I'm the listener? What if I was just somebody walking down the sidewalk?"

"Then you wouldn't be late," he admitted, his round face serious. "But you're not, right? You're my listener."

Quinney nodded and started to sit down next to him.

"Then you're late!" he said, triumphant. "No, wait, wait," he added, just as she was getting comfortable, "get up. I want us to be on the swing when we talk. Don't start your clock, not yet."

"My clock?"

"The fifteen minutes. I get to say when they start and stop, right?"

"You get to say when they start. *I* get to say when they stop. You have the dollar?"

Toby nodded, cramming his hand down in the pocket of his shorts. Quinney could hear the jingle of coins as they walked to the front porch. She felt funny about taking money from such a little kid, but decided business was business.

A screen door opened as they settled back onto the dusty green-and-white-striped canvas cushions of the swing and a woman peered at them. "Toby?" she said. "Do you want to introduce me to your friend?"

"This is . . . Tabby," the little boy said. He turned to Quinney. "That's my mom."

"Do you kids want some lemonade? Some graham crackers?" Toby's mother asked. She looked puzzled but was smiling a little, as if wanting to appear friendly.

"No, thanks," Quinney said.

"Me either," Toby said. "But maybe in fifteen minutes."

"*Tabby,*" Quinney said, grinning at him as the screen door clicked shut. "Quick thinking. Okay, so what do you want to talk about?"

"Starting now?"

Quinney looked at her watch. Obviously this kid needed a little ceremony. "Starting—now!" she said, slicing her arm down through the air. It was almost three fifteen; she'd give him a couple of free minutes and listen until three thirty.

Toby stretched out his legs and stared down at his pudgy knees. But he was silent.

I'd better start, Quinney finally thought. "So you're six, right?"

Toby nodded.

"And you're here for the summer?"

He nodded again, miserable.

"You said that you were lonely."

Now he looked like he was going to cry. *Oh, great,* Quinney thought. "You also said something about being advanced," she added, quickly changing the subject.

"I am," he said, brightening. "I mean, not in my spelling and stuff, but other ways. Like music, and math. And I'm learning French. *Bonjour,*" he said.

"*Bonjour* right back at you," Quinney said, laughing.

"Okay, so you're advanced. Not that I was arguing."

"But I *am* lonely," Toby said.

"Like, how?"

"Like, there's no one to play with," he said, as if pointing out the obvious.

"Well, don't you think that's because you're only here for the summer? You don't know any kids in Lake Geneva."

"If there were kids in Lake Geneva, they'd drown," Toby said, starting to smile. "Unless they were very good swimmers."

Quinney laughed, trying to encourage him. "Good one, Toby. But what about what I said? Don't you think that's why you're lonely here?"

"Yeah, but I'm lonely *everywhere*," Toby confessed. "I just notice it more now because it's summer. I don't have so many lessons in the summer. I mean, I have a lot, but not like in the winter," he corrected himself.

He certainly was a good talker, Quinney thought. She couldn't imagine Teddy and Mack expressing themselves as well. "So you're lonely at home, too?" she asked. "Where do you live the rest of the year, anyway?"

"Connecticut. It takes a long time in the car to get here."

"Tell me about your friends at home."

Toby poked at his knees. "Well, Tucker lives next door. He's only four. But he bites," Toby added, suddenly sounding prim. "We decided it's too dangerous for me to play there."

"We did, huh? And what about at school?"

Toby's face brightened a little. "There's Linda," he said. "She likes me. But we can't play after school, ever, because she has lessons, too."

"Lessons?"

"I have piano and math tutoring, and French. Linda has a creative writing workshop, horseback, and dance. On different days than me."

"How old is she? Fifteen?" Quinney teased, a little envious of Linda's activities.

"She's six, too."

Quinney tried to imagine her mother taking the twins all over creation to one lesson after another. She couldn't; her mom believed in as much empty time as possible for kids. Empty, as in *NO TV DURING THE DAY, EVER*. "I want my kids to figure things out for themselves," she always said. "I want them to be creative!" Naturally, Quinney's father agreed.

They always agreed.

"Does your mom have a job?" Quinney asked Toby, curious.

"I'm her job," he said, sounding a little proud.

"What about hobbies? Doesn't *she* take music lessons, or something?"

"I guess I'm her hobby, too," Toby said.

"Well, have you met any kids at all, here in Lake Geneva? *At* Lake Geneva," she quickly corrected herself, before Toby could make another lame joke.

"I met this one kid when I went to the library with my mom. But he got tired of me, I think."

"How come?"

"How come I think that? Because when I asked him if he wanted to come over and listen to me play the piano, he said he had to go home. He said he was already tired of listening to me."

"Oh," Quinney said, "he was tired of *listening* to you. Did you give him a chance to say anything?"

Toby thought, and said, "Well, I tried to teach him some French."

"That's not quite the same thing, Toby. Couldn't you guys just . . . hang out together?"

"I'm not very good at that, I guess," Toby said sadly. "Maybe it's because I'm so advanced."

"Stop saying how advanced you are!" Quinney said, frustrated. "Once is plenty. Maybe it's too much, even! Anyway, Toby, it looks like you're not that advanced at making friends."

Toby frowned, and glared at Quinney from narrowed eyes. "You're supposed to *listen* to me, you're not supposed to criticize me," he said.

Quinney sighed. He was right, really. Here she was, giving advice again. She stood up, and the porch swing creaked and swayed. "Okay, Toby, but your fifteen minutes are up. I have to go home now."

Toby stood up too, and reached glumly into his pocket for some coins. He dumped three quarters, two dimes, a nickel, and some lint into Quinney's hand. "There," he said, staring at the floor. "This was pretty good, I guess. It was okay, anyway."

"Oh, Toby. I'm sorry I criticized you. It's just—it sounds like one of the reasons you're so lonely is that you don't know how to be a friend. But maybe that's not all your fault," she added quickly, thinking of his busy schedule. "You haven't had time to practice much."

"I don't want to be a friend, I want to *have* friends," Toby pointed out.

"Yeah, but first you have to *be* a friend," Quinney repeated. That was what her mom was always telling the twins, anyway.

"Oh," Toby said politely, but clearly he didn't know what she was talking about. After a pause, he asked, "You want some lemonade? I can yell for my mother."

"I can't, Toby. I have to baby-sit my little brothers for a while. My mom and dad are going out."

"You have brothers?" he asked, sounding excited. "How many?"

"Two. They're twins," Quinney said. "Five years old. They're littler than you." She decided not to mention Monty.

"Do you think they want to come over and play?"

"Probably not," Quinney said quickly. Her listening business was a secret, she reminded herself, and something to be kept separate from her family. She intended for it to stay that way, too. "The twins don't like the piano very much, unless they're the ones pounding on it."

"Okay," Toby said, looking sad. Then he brightened again. "Can I ask you something?"

"Sure, go ahead," Quinney said.

"Do you get red hair from eating carrots?" he asked.

Quinney's hand flew up to her hair. "How should I know? My hair is brown," she said.

Toby stared at her forehead. "But do you cut your bangs with a paper cutter? They're in a perfectly straight line."

She tried to ruffle her hair a little. "They're not perfectly straight," she said.

"Yes they are."

"Well, I *don't* use a paper cutter," Quinney said a little grouchily. "And don't you go trying to use one on your hair, either. You could cut off your nose. Like—this!" she added, swooping her hand toward his face. She held up a fist, and her thumb was poking up between her first and second finger, looking a little like the end of a nose.

Teddy and Mack always cracked up over that one.

Sure enough, Toby touched his nose—to make sure it was still there, Quinney guessed—and started giggling. "Well, *au revoir,*" he finally managed to say.

"*Au revoir,* kiddo," Quinney said.

The little boy beamed. "That means we'll see each other again."

"I know," Quinney said. "I'm a little advanced myself."

Chapter Five

Teddy and Mack

The Main Street sidewalks were crowded as Quinney shooed Teddy and Mack along in front of her. They were heading toward Duell's, the twins' favorite hangout. Duell's was a small store tightly packed with comic books, an impressive gum and candy display, a few toys, and Lake Geneva's biggest video selection. There was also a little pharmacy counter way in the back.

"Can we get four videos?" Mack asked, looking over his shoulder at Quinney. His brown hair still stuck up in back from where Teddy had tried to cut it last month, she noticed, hiding a grin. "Monty says we should stay up all night," Mack stated.

The invisible Monty was a definite presence in the Todd household. For example, he didn't like lima beans, so no limas. That was okay with Quinney. But Monty didn't like mushy videos, so no love stories could ever be rented. One on-screen kiss—and the twins started howling on Monty's behalf.

And Monty was sort of sloppy, so the boys' toys were usually scattered all around. Quinney had finally come up with one rule about Monty: No talking about him to anyone outside the family. That would be getting *too* weird, in her opinion.

"Monty knows perfectly well that Mom said only one video for you guys to share," she told her brothers. "And one for me, if I want," she added.

But I *don't* want, Quinney thought, remembering the phone call to Cree that she was going to make at eight o'clock that night. At a little *after* eight, she corrected herself. Who needed a video for entertainment when there was that to look forward to? And then Brynn was coming over at around nine thirty, after she got back from shopping in Peters Falls with her mom. She was going to spend the night.

It will be hard keeping my conversation with Cree a secret from Brynn, but I'll just *have* to, Quinney thought. Anyway, tonight Marguerite would probably be the main topic. She was spending the night at her aunt's house in Saratoga Springs because her parents had had another fight. A hurried "I can't talk now" was all Quinney had gotten out of her that morning on the phone. She still didn't know how that party had gone.

"Watch where you're going," Quinney cautioned

the twins, but Teddy tripped over a crack in the side-walk anyway.

Poor old Lake Geneva, Quinney thought as Teddy and Mack giggled and whispered together, stumbling their way down the block. Even the little town's side-walks were falling apart. Well, it *had* been a rough winter.

The town's most prosperous moment had been more than a hundred years ago, with logs bumping down the Hudson, with the tannery hugging the banks of the river, and with all those dairy farms rolling clear down to the water's edge.

It had been an uglier town in those days, though, Quinney thought. Her mom sometimes dragged her over to the historical society where Mrs. Todd volun-teered one afternoon a month. Quinney would look at old photographs on the wall then, trying to figure out exactly where they'd been taken. She couldn't help liking the way things looked now—even better than the *real* prosperity recorded in the old photographs. But the town didn't *make* anything anymore. It just sat there, waiting for someone to *want* something.

And that was sad.

Yes, it had been uglier town in the old days, Quinney thought, with stubbled hills and the endless blank wooden walls of the tannery, but it had been richer, too. At least everyone in those old pictures seemed to be doing something, seemed to have a job.

A job! Quinney hadn't thought much about jobs before this summer, before she had one of her own. Now that she'd started working herself, her job was about the most important thing in the world.

"Quit it," Teddy said to his brother, shoving him sideways.

"You quit it," Mack said, not quite daring to push him back.

"You both quit it," Quinney said, "or I'm renting something with lots of hugging in it."

The boys gave each other a look, then started marching down the street stiff-legged, like little toy soldiers. They walked past an old house that now housed a river rafting outfit, a vacant lot, and the Methodist Church's thrift shop.

Quinney resumed her thoughts. A job wasn't just about money, not the way she saw it. She'd always had enough money, what with her allowance, and birthday and Christmas gifts from relatives. She'd saved most of it, too—*just in case,* as she always told herself. But a job was more important than money somehow. It was about working at something and being good at it.

And she *liked* working! Marguerite always said that she was going to marry some rich guy so she could just lie around the pool all day. Either that, or she was going to be a movie star so she could lie around in Hollywood.

Quinney didn't think that either of those things sounded very interesting, at least the lying-around part.

Maybe she liked working because her parents had always worked. Her dad taught school during the school year and worked at Sears in the summer. Her mom taught part-time at a preschool and volunteered, and spent the rest of the time on her art. She had an exhibit coming up in November, and she'd run out of space in her studio, which used to be the Todds' dining room.

But then again, Quinney thought, Marguerite's parents both worked too, so there went that theory. Mr. and Mrs. Harper had full-time jobs, he at the paper mill in nearby Marathon and she at one of the factory outlets in Peters Falls. Mrs. Harper also had that part-time weekend job at the bowling alley.

No one ever seemed to be home over at Marguerite's house, including Marguerite.

Now Teddy and Mack were flinging their arms and legs way out with each step—pretending to be robots, Quinney thought. People were staring. "Cut it out, you guys," Quinney told them.

Maybe how you felt about working depended on

the *kind* of job you had, Quinney thought. She tried to make a mental list of the different jobs she'd heard of. She thought of Spike Ryder, Ms. Ryder's husband. What did he do? Quinney couldn't remember.

Ms. Ryder had told Quinney that *she'd* been laid off from her job at the supermarket in Peters Falls eight months ago and couldn't find work. That couldn't be helping their marriage, Quinney thought. Maybe that was the real reason the Ryders never took a vacation.

Brynn's mom had a part-time job working behind the pharmacy counter at Duell's, and she cleaned houses when she could get the work. I'd *hate* doing that, Quinney thought. I can barely keep my room picked up. But Mrs. Mathers seemed to do okay. She and Brynn lived in a somewhat battered mobile home. Brynnie never complained. Not about money, anyway. She griped more about her mother's rules.

Jobs. When you were a kid, Quinney thought, you didn't think about anyone's job much, as long as you had enough of everything and got a pretty good allowance.

Hey, Quinney thought, I guess this means I'm not such a kid anymore!

"Well, what about some grape gum?" Teddy asked, sidestepping a cluster of tourists eating ice cream cones in front of Papa's, the town's one ice cream shop. Papa's was open only in the summer.

"No," Quinney said. "Monty hates the way it smells, remember?"

"Oh, right," her little brother said.

"So he's not here now?" Quinney asked, smiling.

"He stays home when we go to the store," Teddy said.

"Yeah, ever since he knocked over that video display. They told him never to come back, or he'd be sorry," Mack added. "But he told us to get something with monsters in it."

"I didn't think anyone else knew about Monty," Quinney said, frowning a little. "I told you guys to keep him a secret, remember?"

"Just the video lady knows," Mack assured her. "And we had to tell her, or else me and Teddy would have gotten yelled at. Anyway," he added virtuously, "it's wrong to tell a lie."

"Hmm," Quinney said.

A woman trying to lick the drips from the bottom scoop of a double-dip ice cream cone backed into Quinney. "Oops!" she exclaimed.

"Sorry," Quinney said, jumping back.

"*She* bumped into *you*," Teddy informed her as they continued their journey down the sidewalk.

"It never hurts to be polite," Quinney told him.

"Huh," Teddy said to his brother. "I'm *never* going to be a tourist."

Tourists and ice cream, ice cream and tourists, Quinney thought as they finally neared Duell's. Tourists and ice cream seemed to go together in Lake Geneva, at least during the summer. And with so many tourists, it paid to keep everything pretty in town—which was *good*, Quinney thought.

Barrel planters spilled over with red and white petunias, and even Main Street's several vacant lots were neatly mowed. These open spaces gave the little town a spacious look—misleadingly prosperous, Quinney knew, since the lots were vacant only because no one thought it was worthwhile building anything new. Her dad had told her that. In fact, the only new building in town was the bank, and it had changed hands three times in the last three years.

In front of the town's one realtor, though, a display board fairly bristled with rain-pocked photographs of houses and property for sale—lakefront, riverfront, country, near the school.

The boys were on their best behavior now. The three of them walked past the outdoor display of various newspapers weighted down with bricks and pushed open Duell's heavy glass door. They walked gratefully into the cool air of the store, which was scented with the mingled fragrances of pipe tobacco, squirted perfume samples, and floor wax.

The twins snuffled deep appreciative breaths and darted gleeful looks at each other. Then Teddy's gaze turned toward the candy section. "*This* way," Quinney said, herding them instead in the direction of the videos.

She had limited the twins to the children's section, of course, hoping for a quick getaway, but there were still dozens of titles for the boys to choose from. "What about this?" Mack asked nervously, holding up a display box with cartoon pandas on the front.

"That's for babies," Teddy told him. Mack looked dashed. "But *this* is a good movie," Teddy said, reaching for a box that showed a bad guy grimacing while a little boy held a lighted firecracker under his rear end.

"That looks scary," Mack said, "and if it's too scary we'll have to stop watching it. And then we'll have *no* video. What about this one?" he ventured, holding another box close to his chest.

"That's for girls," Teddy informed him. Mack's lower lip quivered.

At this rate, Quinney thought, the twins would *never* make up their minds. "Okay, okay," she told them. "You guys can get two videos. Mom said we could, after all, and I guess I don't want one. So you each get to choose one. *One,*" she repeated. "And no arguing."

"I told you," Teddy said, grinning at his brother.

Quinney fixed the boys macaroni and cheese for dinner, their favorite. She made them eat some carrot sticks too, though, take showers, and change into their pajamas before letting them come back downstairs to watch the first video. It was all a matter of organization, she had discovered.

"You can brush your teeth while it rewinds," she told them, "then you can watch the other video. We'll flip a coin to see which one to put on first," she added, before *that* argument could start.

"Rewinding videos is a big waste of time," Mack said.

"So is brushing your teeth. Right, Monty?" Teddy said, addressing an empty corner of the room.

"Monty has teeth?" Quinney asked.

"How do you think he ate all those carrot sticks?" Teddy asked.

Finally the twins were settled and had begun to watch the first video. Quinney wiped the kitchen counter for the third time, squinting for smears. She rearranged the dishes in the draining rack, from little to big, and dared herself not to look at the clock again until it was after eight. She lost.

It was seven fifty-five. She had to wait at least fifteen more minutes before calling Cree. I can't believe I'm actually going to do it, she thought. Oh, if only she could tell someone!

But no, Quinney thought, frowning. She had promised Cree that their conversation would be private and confidential.

Quinney ran her fingertip over the phone's receiver. She scraped off a bit of peanut butter. *One of the twins,* she thought.

She waited.

She thought about Cree.

Chapter Six

Cree

Cree Scovall was two years older than Quinney and her friends, but they had all become intensely aware of him during the last two months of the school year—especially after his little sister's near-accident.

He was a tall, thin kid with shaggy brown hair and dark eyes. There were better athletes at Adirondack Middle School, Quinney knew, although Cree had already started to make a name for himself on the baseball field, and there were probably smarter guys and funnier ones, and maybe even better-looking ones. But Cree combined strong and smart and funny in a way that made everyone want to watch him. Quinney did, anyway, though she'd never told a soul.

Marguerite had guessed, of course. She *would*—it was as though she had special guy-radar, or something.

Cree didn't seem to care about the effect he had on people, which was another great thing about him, in Quinney's opinion. He didn't even notice! He wasn't stuck-up at all—you could just tell.

Quinney could also tell he had never spent an hour at the bathroom mirror, staring at his face, wondering what was wrong with it. But Quinney had done that, lots of times. Cree had never changed his clothes three times before going outside just to water the stupid lawn, or something. Quinney had done that, too.

Maybe it was just girls, she thought gloomily.

He didn't have a girlfriend yet, not one that Quinney had heard about, but she knew he hung out a lot with different groups of kids. Everyone seemed to like him.

And he had something *private* he wanted to talk about to Quinney. Not that he knew it was Quinney.

What time was it, anyway?

She picked up the phone and dialed.

"Hello?"

"Hello, C?"

"Yeah, it's me."

"This is Qui—uh, I mean, this is the professional listener calling back. Is now a good time to talk?"

"It's good. Um . . ." There was silence on the phone for a few seconds. Nervous, Quinney wanted to say something, anything, but she bit her lower lip and waited. Cree was paying her to listen, not talk.

Sure enough, he started to speak again. "Hey," he said, "I'm not sure if this is such a good idea after all."

"Why not?"

"I mean, it's kind of weird, isn't it?"

"Well, lots of people write in to newspaper columns for advice. That's kind of weird too, isn't it?" Quinney asked, echoing his question.

"I guess that's one way to look at it," Cree said, not sounding convinced.

"Maybe you should give it a try. It's only a dollar," Quinney said. She wanted to scream, *Hey, I'll listen for free!* but she resisted the urge. After all, this was supposed to be her summer job. Job, as in money.

"Okay," Cree decided aloud. He took a deep breath, then said, "Look, here's the deal. There was this party the other night, okay? Well, not really a party, it was just some kids hanging out. Mostly high school, maybe one or two a little younger. But mostly high school," he repeated.

"How old are you, C?" Quinney asked, already knowing the answer. He was fourteen. But it seemed like the right thing to ask.

"Um, sixteen," Cree said.

You big fibber, Quinney thought, trying not to laugh.

"Anyway," Cree went on, "there were these guys

there—friends of mine?" He spoke as if he were asking a question, but Quinney knew he wasn't.

"Mmm?" she said, making a listening noise.

"Well, we're *kind* of friends. So they were just kicking back, relaxing and stuff. You know," he said.

"Mmm?" Quinney said.

"Anyway, they saw this girl. You know?"

"This girl. Right."

"And she was really cute, right? But they didn't know her, they didn't know where she came from."

"You mean she just appeared out of nowhere?"

"Sort of. It was dark, and everything. Well, there was a full moon," Cree said, remembering, "but it was still pretty dark."

"Wait a minute," Quinney said. "You mean, this was outside?"

"Right, the party was outside—on Mahoney's Hill. I thought I said."

"No." Quinney's heart was starting to pound, hard; she almost expected to see it popping from her chest, cartoon-style.

"Well, anyway, so this girl came up to one of these guys, one of my friends, and she was all talking to him, and stuff. Joking with him. Like she liked him?"

"Mmm?" Could Cree really be talking about who she *thought* he was talking about?

60

"Anyway, so she finally left," Cree continued. "By herself, I think, I'm not sure. But these other guys, the ones that were with my friend, they started teasing him. You know, about this girl. How she liked him, and everything?"

"Mmm?"

"So this other girl, she's in high school, she heard them laughing and stuff. And she says this girl—the one who just appeared out of nowhere—*she* says she's just a kid. That she was in fifth grade last year."

Marguerite, Quinney thought. It *had* to be.

"Hello?" Cree said. "You still there?"

"I'm here," Quinney said grimly. "The high school girl said this mystery girl was in the fifth grade."

"Yeah," Cree said. "So that just made everything worse, right? About the teasing, I mean. Everyone was just laying it on this poor guy, the one that girl flirted with. Really ripping into him, you know?"

"Mmm?" Quinney said. It was better than screaming *Arghhh,* anyway.

"So, this guy? He starts laughing, like it's all a big joke. But I can tell he's kind of mad at this girl, the one who left, the fifth grader. He feels like an idiot, right? She made him look like a fool. She was just a kid, see," he explained.

"If that high school girl was right," Quinney said.

61

"Huh?"

"If she was right about this girl being in fifth grade last year," Quinney said.

"She was right," Cree said gloomily.

"How do you know?"

"This other guy recognized her—he's seen her at the bowling alley. Her mom works there sometimes, I guess. That's what he said, anyway."

It *was* Marguerite. Quinney could barely keep from groaning aloud.

"So anyway, this guy—my friend—he decides he wants to get even with this girl. For crashing the party."

Oh, no, Quinney thought, twisting the phone cord around and around her wrist until her hand started to turn white. "He wants to get even?" she asked. "How?"

"By teaching her a lesson this weekend."

"This weekend?"

"There's another party."

"But how does he know he'll see her then?" Quinney asked, trying to keep her voice calm.

"She said she'd be back," Cree said.

"And you're worried," Quinney said, as if stating a fact.

"Well, yeah. I mean, this poor little kid! First place, what was she even doing there? Only older kids get to hang there. And second, what if she gets hurt this weekend?"

Quinney gritted her teeth. She felt a twinge of jealousy that Cree was trying to protect Marguerite—who had been a dope, after all, going all alone to that party. But she was more worried for her friend than she was jealous. "You think this guy is actually going to hurt her?" she asked.

"Well, not on purpose, anyway. But he's got this motorbike, and he said he's going to tell her to get on. Then he's going to give her a ride she'll never forget—the ride of a lifetime, up and down those trails. She could get hurt real easy up there in the dark."

It was true, Quinney realized—the dirt trails on Mahoney's Hill were almost vertical in places.

"Even if she doesn't get hurt," Cree went on, "she'll probably be scared to death. And every kid within a ten-mile radius of Lake Geneva is going to hear about her getting all humiliated and everything. This could really wreck her."

"It sure could," Quinney said. Marguerite acted tough, but she would never get over something like this. Never. She'd probably end up running away, Quinney thought.

"But these guys are my friends!" Cree went on. "I feel bad ratting on them. And I don't even know this girl. So what am I supposed to do?"

"Do you know who she is? Her name?"

"Margery, Margaret. Something like that. I don't know," he said, sounding frustrated.

"Maybe you can warn her, tell her not to show up next weekend," Quinney suggested.

"Is that what you're advising me to do, warn her?" Cree asked. "But how? And what about my friends? Don't I owe some loyalty to them?"

"Maybe . . . maybe it's kind of like a math problem," Quinney said, thinking suddenly of her father. He was always saying how everyday things could often be reduced to mathematical equations.

"*Math?*" Cree said.

"You know," Quinney gabbled, "like weighing stuff. You could figure that this girl might get hurt on the trails much more than your friend was hurt at the party. It doesn't come out equal. But I'm not advising you, not really," she added.

"Oh, I thought you were," Cree said.

"No, I'm a listener, not an advice-giver."

Cree didn't speak for a moment or two. "Well, I guess my time is about up," he finally said, sighing. "I'll mail you the dollar."

He had hated talking to her. Quinney just *knew* it. "No, wait—wait a minute," she said. "Your watch must be fast. There's a minute or two left. What are you going to do? Have you decided?"

"I don't know. Go to the bowling alley? Try to find her before the party?" Cree sounded as if he were trying to pass a pop quiz—or answer a question right, just so he could hang up.

"That's a good idea," Quinney said, trying to encourage him. "When exactly is the next party, anyway?"

"Saturday. They're always on Saturdays during the summer, unless it's raining."

"Well, why don't you try the bowling alley on Friday night?"

"I don't know about that," Cree said, sounding reluctant. "Look," he blurted out, "I didn't even say for sure that I was going to try to talk to this girl! I mean, she did something stupid, right? What happens next is her own fault. Why should *I* always have to be the one to fix things?"

Quinney almost gasped. Cree feels that way, too? she thought, amazed.

"Are you still listening?" he asked.

Quinney cleared her throat. "I'm listening," she said. "But look," she added suddenly. "Just because Mar— I mean that *girl* did something stupid, that doesn't mean you shouldn't help her if you can. Hey, didn't *you* ever do anything stupid?" she added, trying to tease.

"Yeah," he muttered, and Quinney could almost hear the unspoken end to his thought: *Like when I answered your crazy ad.*

"Well, okay then," Quinney said, trying not to cringe. "Maybe you could talk to your friend, try to change his mind," she added, trying to keep him on the phone. She could tell he was about to hang up.

"Yeah, right," Cree said.

It was obvious *that* was never going to happen.

"Uh—I have to go," Cree said politely, "but thanks. I might write you another card, make another appointment. This wasn't so bad. It *was* confidential, though, right? You promised."

"Oh, right. Totally private and totally confidential. Right," Quinney said automatically.

But was this a promise she could keep? Was it one she *should* keep?

"Okay. Well, good-bye, uh, listener," Cree said. "And thanks. Maybe you even helped."

"I hope so. That's what I'm here for. Good-bye, Cree," Quinney said.

And could have died on the spot.

She'd said *Cree.*

Talk about stupid.

"What?" Cree almost shouted.

"What, what?" Quinney asked, her heart pounding.

"You said my name! You called me *Cree*. Who *is* this?" Cree demanded. "Do I know you?"

"I didn't call you that," Quinney lied. "I never said *Cree*, I said C! 'Good-bye, C.' You must have heard me wrong!"

"Huh," Cree said. Quinney could almost see his eyes narrow with suspicion.

"Look, I have to hang up now," she said. "But I promise you don't know me." She placed the telephone receiver carefully on its hook.

And I guess you never will, she thought.

Chapter Seven

Brynn

Brynn's knock on the Todds' front door at nine thirty that night was so gentle, Quinney almost didn't hear it. She'd told Brynn not to ring the doorbell, though, because Teddy and Mack would be in bed.

Quinney ran down the stairs when she heard the knock. She hurried to the door and peeked out through the window at the top. Brynn seemed to be looking down at her shoes; her blond hair looked almost white under the porch light. The thing that Quinney most wanted to tell her friend—*Guess who I've been talking on the phone with for the last twenty minutes?*—was the one thing she couldn't say. Quinney didn't really know how she was going to keep her mouth shut about it. But she had to, she told herself—people trusted her.

She opened the door.

"Aah—you scared me," Brynn said, jumping back a little, then laughing at herself.

"Who did you think I was," Quinney teased, "the terrible twins?"

"No, no, anything but that!" Brynn said. She was joking, but she usually made it a point to show up at Quinney's after the boys had gone to bed. She looked cautiously around the front hall. "They *are* asleep, aren't they?"

"Don't worry—you're safe," Quinney said. Brynn didn't have any brothers or sisters, and the twins made her nervous. They, on the other hand, thought she was wonderful; Quinney had noticed that her softness, her pink-and-whiteness seemed to stun them into silence. It was as if they thought Brynn was a fairy princess.

They *never* would have gone to bed if they'd known Brynn was coming over, Quinney thought, leading her friend into the kitchen. She grinned, imagining the looks on the boys' faces in the morning when they saw Princess Brynn eating cereal at their own kitchen table. "Want to nuke up some popcorn?" she asked, opening a cellophane packet.

"Sure," Brynn said happily. "Microwaves are so great. I wish we had room for one."

"Well, I like fixing popcorn at your house on the stove," Quinney said. "I think it tastes better popped in a black iron pan." She punched a few buttons, and the microwave started to whir.

"But it's a mess to clean up," Brynn said. "Want me to make the lemonade?"

"Sure. I can never get rid of that big icy lump when I stir," Quinney said. The microwave beeped.

Brynn got a can of lemonade concentrate from the Todds' freezer, opened it, and let the concentrate fall into a glass pitcher with a plop. "Better open the popcorn bag in your room, with the door shut," Brynn advised, filling the can with water. "Remember last time? Mack smelled it in his sleep and practically flew downstairs." She rinsed her hands at the sink, looked around for a towel, and then wiped them on her Levi's.

"Oh yeah," Quinney said, laughing. She held the swinging door open with her shoulder for Brynn, who was carrying the pitcher and two glasses, and the girls tiptoed out of the kitchen, giggling and shushing each other.

Quinney's bedroom was upstairs, as was the twins' room and a guest room, which used to be Mr. and Mrs. Todd's room. But Quinney's parents had built a master bedroom addition onto the first floor of their house a few years earlier, so the kids had the top floor to themselves.

Quinney's was the first room at the top of the stairs. She and her mom had painted over the old Raggedy Ann wallpaper the summer before. Now the room was a pretty peach color, with glossy white trim. White curtains with ball fringe framed both windows, and white chenille bedspreads—strewn with throw pillows and old stuffed animals—covered Quinney's twin beds. One of her mother's landscape paintings of a field near the river hung between the windows, and three faded rag rugs warmed the floor. Quinney loved her room.

"So how was shopping?" Quinney asked when they'd quietly shut her bedroom door behind them. "Get anything good?" She shoved some stuffed animals onto the floor and sat down on one of the beds, tugging the popcorn bag open and sniffing the escaping steam with appreciation.

Brynn sat down on the other bed. She leaned over and grabbed a handful of popcorn, washing it down with some lemonade before she answered. "Oh, you know the outlets," she finally said. "My mom says that everything's twice as expensive as at real stores. She says outlets are just a scam for tourists."

"Yeah," Quinney said, chewing, "but we don't *have* any real stores around here. So we're stuck." Even Peters Falls was a half hour away. And to get there, you had to endure what every Lake Geneva kid considered to be a boring drive along a curving two-lane road, past several lakes and about a billion trees. Tourists called it scenic, but they didn't need to drive it to get anywhere.

"Well, that's okay with me," Brynn said, "because we couldn't afford to buy anything anyway."

Quinney didn't know what to say to that.

"My mom did get me some nice socks, though," Brynn told Quinney. "That's me," she added, laughing, "designer socks!" She held out her foot. Tiny, pink-uddered cows marched around her ankle.

"You're famous for wearing cute socks," Quinney reassured her.

Brynnie sighed, looking down at the cows. "Where'd your parents go this time?" she asked suddenly. She often asked about them, Quinney had noticed.

"To the baseball game in Peters Falls," Quinney said, shrugging. "Why?"

Brynn blushed pinker than usual. "Oh, I don't know—I just wondered, that's all. I didn't know your mom liked baseball."

Quinney thought for a moment. "I don't think she likes baseball or doesn't like it," she finally said. "My dad either, really. They just like going places together." Without us kids, she thought. It had gotten worse over the summer.

Brynn sighed. "Well," she said, with a faraway look on her face, "I think it's romantic. I just hope my husband and I are like that, when we get married. You know, madly in love."

Yuck, Quinney thought, chomping fiercely on a mouthful of popcorn. Who wanted to think about their parents being madly in love? Sick! She reached over to the night table for her glass of lemonade and took a long, noisy drink. "So when are you going to get married?" Quinney teased, hoping to change the subject. "Anytime soon?"

Brynn sneaked a sideways look at Quinney. "Nope. Not as soon as Marguerite is—I mean, not at the rate she's going," she said. She ducked her head and stared at the floor, trying to hide a sly smile.

Quinney tossed a piece of popcorn into the air to hide her confusion, and she tried to catch it in her mouth. It bounced off her cheek and disappeared under the bureau.

Brynn didn't usually criticize Marguerite this way. What was going on? Had Brynnie and Marguerite had another fight and not told her about it?

"That's not a very nice thing to say, *dear,*" she finally remarked in a high, squeaky voice, mimicking a Campfire Girl leader they used to have. "Be sweet, now."

"Oh, I'm sweet as pie," Brynn squeaked back. "But I'm telling the truth," she added in her normal voice.

"What are you saying, Brynn?" Quinney asked flatly. "That Marguerite is going to fall in love, get married, and have a baby with some guy she meets at a party she crashes?"

Brynn raised her head and stared at Quinney. "Well," she said, "not necessarily in that order. The stork might beat the minister, as my mom would say. But yeah, basically. Why not? That's what happens to a lot of the girls around here, isn't it? Year after year?"

Quinney didn't know what to say. Why was Brynn dumping on Marguerite? The three of them had known one another forever.

Maybe she's worried that I like Marguerite better than I like her, Quinney thought suddenly.

Three girls being best friends was hard. It reminded Quinney again of her father's theory about ordinary things being reduced to mathematical equations.

Maybe two into three didn't *go*. Not when you were almost teenagers, anyway.

But there had been lots of times in the past when Brynn and Marguerite hung out together and Quinney had felt like the outsider. Couldn't Brynn see that when three kids were friends, everything always evened out sooner or later?

Nothing had to change—not *really*.

"So you're just going to listen? You're not going to talk to me?" Brynn asked, trying to sound casual. She picked up a floppy sock doll and examined it closely, as if she'd never seen it before.

"Well, I think you're wrong about Marguerite getting married young," Quinney finally said. "The last thing she wants is to get stuck *here* for the rest of her life. She wants adventure, romance."

"People always say that, but look where they end up," Brynn pointed out. "What do you think happened to my mom?"

"To your mom?" Quinney asked, confused. Why were they talking about Brynnie's mother all of a sudden?

"Yeah," Brynn said, scowling a little. She twisted some hair around her finger as she spoke. "She had big plans, too—until she got pregnant with me, anyway, and married her stupid boyfriend, my wonderful father, who then dumped her."

Quinney's breath seemed to catch in her throat. Brynnie had never talked about her father before. In fact, Quinney didn't know whether or not Brynn had ever met him.

"Mom told me all about it once," Brynn continued, looking as if she was still listening to her mother's words. "Before that happened, she wanted to move to California and study to be a nurse."

Quinney cleared her throat. "I never knew that," she said.

Brynn flashed her a look of contempt. "What, did you think that her big dream was to live all alone with her daughter in a beat-up trailer, work part time in a drugstore, and clean other people's houses?"

"But—but—you never said you guys were unhappy," Quinney sputtered. "Come on, be fair—I didn't know."

"*Your* mom and dad didn't get married in high school, did they?" Brynn asked.

"No," Quinney admitted.

"And they waited to have you and the twins until they were good and ready to, didn't they?" she went on.

"I guess." Quinney didn't feel like trying to explain to Brynn how alone and out of place she felt *anyway*, despite her parents' happy marriage.

"That's all I'm saying," Brynn said, flapping her arms helplessly. "It just drives me *crazy* how every girl who's ever born in this town thinks she'll be different, thinks she'll get away and *do* something. And then the same thing happens, over and over again."

"And you think it's going to be like that for Marguerite," Quinney stated. She thought of what Cree had told her. Maybe Brynn's *right*, she thought, a hollow feeling in her throat.

But what could she do?

"Sure it'll be like that. Why not?" Brynn asked. "She made all the right moves so far. Like she was following directions on a map." Brynn leaned forward urgently. "You have to really *work* at it to be different, Quinney. Marguerite is just like my mom was, don't you see? Exactly! The rate she's going, she'll get pregnant in a couple of years, and then boom—her story will be over."

"It wouldn't be *over* over if she got pregnant, Brynn. She'd still have the rest of her life to live, and a baby to love."

"Just like my mom, right?" Brynn asked, her voice bitter. "Not that she doesn't love me. I don't mean that," she added. She shook her head slowly and gave Quinney a helpless look, like she'd said more than she'd wanted.

"Brynn, I—"

"God, Quinney," Brynn interrupted, "you're just about the smartest person I know, but sometimes you can't see what's right in front of your face, can you?"

"I never said I was all that smart," Quinney mumbled, feeling dumber by the minute. "And anyway," she added, "why don't you talk to Marguerite yourself if you think she's making such a big mistake instead of telling *me* about it?" She was especially glad now that she hadn't told Brynn about Cree's phone call. Brynn

77

would only have used it against Marguerite.

"Oh, Quinney—wake up!" Brynn said, sounding disgusted. "I haven't known what to say to Marguerite for almost a year. We're only friends anymore because we both like you."

Quinney didn't want to hear this. "That's not true," she said. "If you can't talk to her, I'm sure it's just a temporary thing."

Brynn stared at her. "Can't you see how much Marguerite has changed lately?" she finally asked, saying each word slowly.

"I guess, maybe a little," Quinney admitted. "But we're changing too, Brynn. We can all change together! And I still think you're wrong about what's going to happen to Marguerite."

"Well, maybe," Brynn said, stretching her arms over her head. She yawned, then added, "One thing's for sure—there's nothing we can do except sit back and watch it all happen."

We'll see about *that*, Quinney thought grimly.

Chapter Eight

Being Lonely

The Lake Geneva Market was unusually crowded for a Wednesday morning. Quinney was doing the shopping for her mom, who was busy painting a picture, and for her dad, who had taken the day off and was attempting to fix a toaster oven that was practically an antique. Both parents were supposedly watching the twins.

Quinney sometimes thought the family needed two or three full-time child-care workers to keep up with Teddy and Mack, but her mom often just put Monty in charge—if Quinney wasn't around. "Monty's going to have to stay in his room if anything big goes wrong," she had warned the twins that morning.

Well, it seems to work, Quinney thought as she scanned the meat section for the least icky chicken parts she could find. She hated it when pink poultry juice got all over her fingers.

"Tabby!" a voice behind her said.

Quinney whirled around. Only two people in the world would call her that.

Sure enough, there was Toby's mother. There was no sign of Toby, though. "Oh, hi," Quinney said.

"Hi there," Mrs. Toby said. That wasn't her name, of course, but that's how Quinney remembered her. "What a coincidence!"

"Yeah," Quinney agreed weakly. "Where's Toby?"

"Home, practicing. My sister's here. She's watching him for me. Uh, Tabby," she said, lowering her voice a little, "do you think I could talk with you for a minute? Privately?"

"Sure," Quinney said. "It's usually pretty quiet over there by the kibble." They pushed their carts toward the towering sacks of dog food in the corner of the store and made a secluded island of themselves behind it. "What did you want to talk about?" Quinney asked, nervous. Why did Mrs. Toby want to speak in private?

"Well, it's about Toby. I just think it's so nice that you two are friends, Tabby."

"I really don't know him all that well. I mean, he's only, what, six?"

"And a half," his mother said, nodding. "But you *did* come over for a visit."

"That's true," Quinney said, not wanting to explain her listening business to Toby's mom.

Anyway, her appointments were supposed to be confidential.

"Well, the thing is," Toby's mom continued, "I was—well, I was in the living room when you and Toby were talking on the porch." She fidgeted with her straw bag, snapping and unsnapping it.

"Mmm?" Quinney said, glad that she'd discovered a good, all-purpose listening noise.

"Well, the point is, Tabby, the window was open. Just a little. You know how hot it's been." *Snap.*

"It's been hot," Quinney agreed, but now she was starting to get really nervous.

"So the thing is, I—I overheard part of your conversation with Toby, the part where you said that maybe being lonely wasn't all his fault. That maybe he just hadn't had a chance to practice making friends." *Snap.*

"But I didn't mean it as a criticism of *you*," Quinney began.

"I know, I know, but it got me thinking. Maybe I didn't schedule enough peer contact for Toby when he was younger."

"Peer contact?" Quinney asked. "Oh, you mean like playing with kids his own age?"

"That's right. But he never seemed to miss it. People have always said talking to Toby is like talking with another adult," she said proudly. "He *liked* being around adults, Tabby. He still does."

"But little kids still need to hang out together," Quinney said. She thought of the twins and Monty sitting under some tree, whispering, arguing, laughing. She pictured them playing with toy cars, stones, or even sticks and leaves, often with one or two other neighborhood kids. Like the Sansom girls, even though they were a year or two older.

Maybe Mom and Dad don't have such weird ideas about raising kids after all, Quinney thought.

"Hang out together?" Mrs. Toby asked. "You mean with a play group?"

"I guess a play group is okay sometimes," Quinney said, frowning. "Usually hanging out just happens, though. Like with my brothers, uh, Timmy and Tommy. They're twins."

"Timmy and Tommy and Tabby. You all have such cute names!"

Oh, we're cute all right, Quinney thought, grimacing a little. She tugged at her short denim skirt. There seemed to be about a mile between its hem and her big knobby knees, she thought gloomily.

"Well," Mrs. Toby said, "I'll give it some thought. Toby's definitely gifted, and it might be hard to plan activities for children who don't, um, share similar interests."

"But the point is *not* to plan activities for them. Let the kids play all by themselves," Quinney said, kicking away a few stray lumps of kibble. "And they don't have to have the same interests. Toby can learn to play what the other kids want to, sometimes."

"Maybe," Mrs. Toby said doubtfully. "Say, I've got an idea," she said, smiling brightly. "Why don't you bring Timmy and Tommy over for a play session some morning? Say, at ten fifteen. That's when Toby finishes his piano practice. Perhaps he could play for everyone. You could all stay for lunch, too—we speak French during meals. It'll be fun! How old are the boys, did you say?"

I *didn't* say, Quinney thought, trying to imagine Teddy and Mack sitting still for a piano recital and French. No way was she bringing them over to Toby's house! Her whole family would find out about her listening job if she did.

"My brothers are kind of little," Quinney finally said, being evasive.

"Oh, that's too bad," Mrs. Toby said. "It would have been such fun."

"Yeah. But maybe there are some kids Toby's age

who could come play with him," Quinney said. It was probably hopeless to suggest skipping the piano and the French, she thought.

"Well, I'll look into it. After all, Toby's social skills are an important part of his development, too," Mrs. Toby said.

Gee, Quinney thought, it's a little late to start thinking about *that*, isn't it? But she gritted her teeth, smiled, and nodded as she wheeled her wobbly grocery cart away.

That woman didn't hear a word I said, Quinney fumed. What a waste of time! She should send *Mrs. Toby* a listening bill. Poor little kid . . .

Parents! Quinney eyed her own curiously the rest of the morning, as if she were a nature scientist.

Her father finally came up from the basement wearing his riverboat captain's cap, followed by the twins. He held the battered toaster oven aloft like a trophy and announced that it was fixed at last. Not only that, they would all have cheese sandwiches for lunch— heated in that very oven!

Quinney wondered why he bothered. This was how he spent his day off? He had wasted the whole morning repairing something he'd found at a yard sale when they already had a toaster oven that worked. He would probably end up giving it away, like all the others.

Now, Quinney noted, Teddy and Mack had drifted out into the backyard and were whispering under the birch tree together. When they weren't following their dad around, they were usually off in their own world with Monty.

Oh, sure, Quinney thought, other kids came over to play, and the twins had made friends in preschool. They'd probably make new ones in kindergarten too. But so far, in spite of what she had implied to Mrs. Toby, all the twins really needed was each other, and the secrets they shared.

Next, Quinney thought about her mother, who was still in the dining room, painting. The swinging door between that room and the kitchen was firmly closed, but the scent of turpentine seeped into the kitchen. "When that door is shut, just think of it as a brick wall," her mother had always told the kids. "You can only knock if it's an emergency. That means *bleeding*," she had stressed.

Her mom seemed to love them so much, and she was crazy about her husband, so why did she shut herself away from them all whenever she could? Sometimes Quinney felt that she barely saw her mother at all. Not alone, anyway.

It didn't make any sense.

Quinney climbed the stairs, cleared off her bed with one sweep of her hand, and then flopped down and thought some more about her family. She clasped a patchwork pillow to her chest as she watched dust motes rise and swirl in a patch of sunlight. Where do I fit in? she wondered. Maybe I'm like the invisible part of a machine that keeps everything else running smoothly.

It felt good to be needed, Quinney admitted to herself, but it wasn't very much fun. What would it take to get some attention?

She should ask Marguerite. Marguerite *demanded* attention, whatever she did.

Marguerite would never be lonely, at least.

"Quinney! I need you!" her mother's voice called from downstairs.

Chapter Nine

This Great Relationship

"**M**om, I can't!" Quinney cried, slamming the silverware drawer shut. "I just baby-sat last night."

"It's only for a couple of hours," her mother said.

"It'll take three hours at least," Quinney argued. "It takes more than an hour just to drive to Saratoga Springs and back. And once Daddy starts looking at those old books you'll never get him to leave."

"I will, Quinney—I promise. And anyway, Mr. Durand has set aside the things he especially wants your dad to look at. Come on, honey—your father took the day off work just for this," she coaxed.

Quinney folded her arms and glared at her mother. "You *know* what's going to happen," she said. "And I already told you, I have to stop by the library this afternoon before it closes."

"Well, run over there now, then!" her mother said. "I'll finish putting the dishes away, and then we'll leave when you get back."

"I can't go now," Quinney grumbled. But there was no *way* she could explain that she had a listening appointment at a quarter to five.

Mrs. Todd held up her hands, helpless. "Quinney, what do you want from me? I only asked you to baby-sit the twins. I wasn't suggesting that you adopt them."

"But you might as well! I take care of them all the time, don't I?" Quinney didn't usually talk to her mother like this, but today, it felt good.

Mrs. Todd blinked, startled.

"At least this summer I have," Quinney said, not wanting to back down.

The door leading to the hallway opened with a *swoosh*, and Quinney's dad burst into the kitchen. "Are you ready to go?" he asked his wife, a big smile on his face.

Mrs. Todd cleared her throat and tilted her head in Quinney's direction. "Norman, I don't know if—"

"Oh, go ahead and go," Quinney said. Suddenly she didn't want to be a spoilsport anymore. "Just be back by four thirty, that's all I ask."

Jeez. It's like talking to a couple of kids, she thought.

At four forty-seven, Quinney was sitting in the library next to the dictionary, trying to catch her breath as she waited for Sam to appear. Her face was a little pale, and her nose was still stuffed up from crying.

On the way out the back door she had yelled at her mom as she was arriving home predictably late from Saratoga Springs. Her father had missed the fight, absorbed as he was with the two new books he'd purchased for his collection, and her mother was too shocked to answer her.

I'm probably the last person in the world who should be giving advice to anyone, she thought gloomily, blowing her nose. But Sam sounded easy. She ought to be able to handle *this* appointment, at least.

If he ever showed up. Thank goodness he was late.

Quinney heard a murmur from the front desk and straightened in her chair. Someone had entered the library, she could tell. Sure enough, a shaggy head peeked around the corner of the reference room a moment later. He tapped at one ear, a questioning look in his eye. Quinney nodded and mimed, *Yes, I am the listener,* tapping her ear, so he joined her at the golden varnished table.

Sam was younger than Quinney had thought he would be, having judged by his telephone voice that he was at least eighty. In person, though, he looked about her father's age, or maybe a little older.

How weird, she thought suddenly, to give advice to

somebody old enough to be a father, not to mention a grandfather.

But no, she corrected herself, *I'm <u>not</u> here to give advice. I'm only supposed to listen. And listening should be easy with Sam.* He wanted to talk.

"So," Sam said happily. "May I ask your name? Or is that not allowed?"

"No, it's okay. My name is Quinney. I'm only twelve, but I've had lots of listening experience already." *A little more than I'd wanted, even,* she added to herself, thinking of Cree.

"Quinney! An unusual name. Now, Sam is an ordinary name," he said. "You might even call it a *common* name, but you'd be surprised how few Sams you'll meet from one week to the next. Tell me, did you meet any other Sams last week?"

"Well, no, I guess I—"

"My point exactly! Not that names have much to do with anything. Well, I guess they do if you have a really unusual one. That could affect the course of your life, for good or bad. I knew this one woman, and her mother had named her Petite. That means 'little' in French."

"I know," Quinney said, thinking she should introduce this guy to Toby. They could jabber away together in French. Mrs. Toby could serve lemonade. "I—"

"Maybe Petite was really tiny or something when she was born. But when I knew her, she was huge! Imagine having to go through life with everyone calling you Petite, when you're so big."

"That would be—"

"And there was this guy I knew named Rocky," Sam interrupted. "This was before the movie. You see those movies? They're all out on video."

Quinney nodded, not attempting to answer him this time. Why try?

"Anyway, even before the movie came out, this guy didn't look like a Rocky. He was this little tiny guy, a brain. You had to laugh. It was like, 'Rocky? Can I borrow your slide rule?' This was in the days when they *had* slide rules. Do they still use them in school?"

"Well, no, they—"

"Because they ought to. You have to learn how to think. I mean, what if a meteor hits us or something? We'll be back in the dark ages before you know it. No one will know how to do anything for himself anymore, figure anything out. Or *herself*," he added, attempting to be fair. "You ever think about that, Quincy?"

"Quinney."

"Whatever. You know, that reminds me of . . ."

On and on, Sam yak-yak-yakked for the next twelve

minutes, while Quinney just sat there. He interrupted her sentences. He interrupted her listening noises. He even interrupted *himself* a couple of times. Finally, Quinney glanced at the clock and noticed with relief that his fifteen minutes were almost up. Pretty soon Mrs. Arbuckle—*I love you, Mrs. Arbuckle!*—would tell them the library was closing for the day.

She sniffed and cleared her throat.

Sam paused, mid-sentence, and asked, "You getting a cold? Because I always say that for a cold, you should—"

But now, Quinney interrupted *him*. "Mr. Weir," she said, "you told me you had some things you wanted to get off your chest."

"Call me Sam. And yeah, I'm getting to those," he said.

Quinney jumped in before he could continue. "Because the thing is, our time is almost up. I mean, it doesn't matter to *me* what you talk about. I'll listen. But I want to make sure you're happy with the appointment when you leave."

"My time is almost up? That's amazing! I'll just have to make another one, then. This has been *fun*!"

Quinney tried not to groan. *Oh, no,* she thought. Fifteen minutes with Sam was like an hour with anyone else.

"But I can tell you in a nutshell what's on my chest," Sam said. "My girlfriend, Cynthia, left me for no good reason. Well, the reason she gave was that I'm too big a slob. It's true that I like things relaxed at my house. That's why I was late today, in fact—I couldn't find my shoes. She called it messy, though. She said it got her down, whenever she came over. It was like I expected her to clean up after me, she said. But I didn't, Quincy! I just don't *see* the mess anymore."

"How long ago did she break up with you?" Quinney asked, while he was taking a breath. She'd ignore the *Quincy* this time.

"A month ago, and I've barely shared a word with anyone since—except at work, over in Peters Falls, and that doesn't count. I'm the boss there. They *have* to listen to me. That's why this has been so great."

"That's why *what* has been so great?" Quinney asked.

"*This*, our conversation."

"But this wasn't a conversation," Quinney blurted out. She couldn't help herself. The guy irritated her!

"What do you mean? Of course it was," he said, looking surprised.

"No, it wasn't. You talked and I listened. That isn't conversation. In conversation, both people talk, and both people listen."

"You talked," he said, puzzled.

"I tried to, but even *that* was just when you said something first."

"But, but . . . I thought that was your job, to listen," Sam said, still confused.

Quinney sighed. "You're right. I'm sorry."

"No, that's okay," Sam said quickly. "In fact, you know something?"

"What?" Quinney asked. She could see Mrs. Arbuckle working her way toward them. *Here we are, Mrs. Arbuckle. Yoo-hoo, over here!*

"Cynthia said that, too. She said, 'Sam, you never shut up long enough to let me get a word in edgewise.' And I was thinking we had this great relationship going! I thought she was just being critical. Looking for another excuse to split, you know?"

"Mmm?" Quinney said.

"But maybe she was right," he said, excited. "I mean, if you notice it too, maybe she had a point."

"Maybe she did," Quinney said encouragingly. Poor Cynthia, she thought.

"And if she was right about that, maybe she was right about me being a slob, too," Sam said. "I could be, you know? It's probably like B.O. You don't notice it on yourself."

"B.O.?" Quinney asked.

"Body odor," Sam whispered. "Anyway, maybe I should clean things up. Maybe Cynthia would come back to me then. I just don't know where to begin."

"Well, I could recommend a good cleaning lady if you're interested," Quinney said. Brynn's mom was always looking for extra work. . . .

"Brynn, it's Quinney."

"Oh, hi, Quinney."

"You eating dinner?"

"Not yet. Mom isn't home. I made some chili, though. Why? You want to come over?"

"Sure, or you could come over here," Quinney said. "You want to spend the night again?"

As if by silent agreement, neither girl mentioned Marguerite.

"I can't, not tonight. I've got to help my mom on a job in the morning," Brynn said. She hesitated. "I guess I could come over for a *little* while, though. What time?"

"Oh, like at eight? Teddy and Mack should be unconscious by then."

"I'll be there at eight thirty, just to be on the safe side," Brynn said.

"Good. See you—oh, and Brynnie? I think I have a lead on another cleaning job for your mom if she's interested."

"I can answer that one. She's interested, for *sure*."

Quinney hung up the phone. It seemed weird not to invite Marguerite over too, but she was still at her aunt's house. And even if she was home, Quinney thought, this new Marguerite would probably think that hanging out with her girlfriends was dumb.

Marguerite *had* changed, Quinney admitted to herself. And what was worse, she thought she was being so cool about everything—when really, she had stepped right into a big mess. Only she didn't know it yet. Only Quinney knew.

I should tell her, Quinney whispered to herself. But what would she say? *Want to come over and bake cookies with me and Brynn, who is practically placing bets on when you're going to ruin your life?*

Yeah, that ought to do it!

And oh, by the way, Marguerite, she could add, *you're going to be totally humiliated on Saturday night by that boy you tried to pick up last weekend. . . .*

No, Quinney thought. She couldn't say those things to her friend—and she couldn't *not* say them, either.

Chapter Ten

Mrs. Todd

"**Y**ou're going to the library *again*?" Mrs. Todd asked Quinney the next afternoon as she patted a meat loaf into shape.

Quinney scrubbed harder at the potatoes she was cleaning. She was still mad at her mom for being late yesterday, for making her baby-sit—for ignoring her one and only daughter. "Yeah, why?" Quinney finally said, her voice cool.

"Well, just look outside," her mother said. She hunched up one shoulder, trying to push back a lock of her long curly hair without touching it.

Quinney gazed out the streaming window. It was raining hard, and thunder boomed in the distance. Summers in Lake Geneva were punctuated by such sudden storms, and living near the water as they did, everyone was wary of lightning. Most people took these storms seriously.

But Quinney shrugged. "I'm not leaving until four thirty," she said. "The storm should be over by then."

And maybe I'll be ready for Ms. Ryder by then, she added to herself.

Quinney's mom washed and dried her hands, put the meat loaf into the refrigerator, then helped herself to an oatmeal cookie while Quinney pricked the potatoes with a fork. Quinney and Brynn had stayed up late baking the cookies.

"You really should go into the cookie business, Quinney," her mother said in her best peacemaking voice. "These are terrific."

Thanks, but I already have a job! Quinney was tempted to say. But she remained silent.

Mrs. Todd hesitated a little. "Are we still fighting?" she finally asked, imitating Mack. That's what he always said to Teddy after a squabble. Mack claimed he could never keep track of whether they were friends or not. Not waiting for an answer, she said, "Quinney," there's something I want to ask you—but I'm almost afraid to, after yesterday."

Quinney rearranged the cookies that were left on the plate. "The fight's over, Mom. Go ahead, ask me."

"Well," Mrs. Todd said, "what about staying home from the library just this once and watching the twins for me?"

Quinney sat down hard and scraped her chair closer to the table. Maybe the fight *wasn't* over, after all.

"I know I've been asking you to sit a lot lately," Mrs. Todd continued, sounding a little embarrassed, "but the thing is, I could really use a couple of hours now in the studio."

Quinney drew an invisible line on the table with her finger.

"You guys could make puppets or something," Mrs. Todd said, trying to make it sound tempting. "It would only be until your father gets back from work, Quinney."

It was that show she was trying to get ready for, Quinney thought. Her mom was nervous about it. Quinney felt sorry for her—*almost.*

"I can't," she said. "Sorry."

Mrs. Todd frowned. "But honey, why not?" she asked. "You're not doing anything special, are you?"

Quinney almost exploded. "Why do you always assume I'm not doing anything special?" she asked, slapping the table so hard that her hand stung. "It's not like I'm the dud in the family!"

"Quinney, I never said—"

"Because as a matter of fact," Quinney interrupted, "I'm going through some really terrible stuff right now." *Wow, just blurt it out,* she berated herself.

"What kind of stuff?" her mom asked, instantly worried. She groped for a kitchen chair, then settled into it.

"Um—well, it's kind of a loyalty thing, like who a person should be loyal to in a certain situation," Quinney said, almost glad to have changed the subject from her afternoon plans. She sat down too, across from her mother.

"Ah, philosophy," her mother said. She started sweeping a few stray lunchtime sandwich crumbs into a tidy pile, using the edge of her hand.

Philosophy, Quinney thought grouchily. Trust her mom to turn a real problem into an intellectual one!

Sometimes it seemed to her that her mother lived in a dream world instead of the one Quinney knew— a world filled with the threat of revenge, possible injury, and certain humiliation. But maybe all artists were like that.

"Quinney?" her mom was saying. "So what's the situation?" She brushed her hands together as if getting ready to tackle any problem, no matter how huge.

"I—I can't really talk about it, Mom. If I did, that would be disloyal to everyone."

Her mother looked worried. "Poor Quinney, you really *are* in a jam, aren't you?" she said. "Well, is there any part of it you *can* talk about? It might help."

Quinney searched her mind for something, some scrap of conversation she could toss to her mother to divert her sudden attention.

But her mom surprised her by saying abruptly, "People really count on you a lot, don't they, Quinney?"

"Uh, I guess."

It was true. They *did*!

"I know *we* all do, anyway," Mrs. Todd continued, "and I'll bet your friends do, too. It must be hard sometimes. After all, you're only twelve."

Yeah, but I'm advanced, Quinney wanted to announce, mimicking Toby. Instead, she said, "It's not so hard."

And for a moment she almost believed what she was saying.

"Well," her mother said with a sigh, "you certainly do have enough common sense for a roomful of ordinary people, Quinney. Just don't forget that even the most practiced professional advice-givers in the world— grown-ups, Quinney—*get* advice on giving advice when there's a problem. *Especially* with questions involving philosophy. They all have someone to talk to."

"What do you mean?" Quinney asked.

"I mean these people always have someone else they can bounce things off. It's a necessity for them."

"I didn't know that," Quinney said. She thought a moment. "But what about secrecy? Privacy?"

"I'm not saying they go blabbing things all around, Quinney," her mother said with a laugh. "It's not like they take out an ad in the paper or something!"

Quinney jumped a little in her creaky chair. Could her mom—no, Mrs. Todd was about the only person in Lake Geneva who never even looked at *Save-a-Cent*, Quinney reassured herself.

"So maybe I'm not the best person to talk to, in this case, anyway," her mom continued reluctantly, "but I hope there's *someone*. Never cut yourself off. You shouldn't have to carry this kind of burden alone, darling."

"Well, you don't have to worry about me being alone," Quinney grumbled, deliberately changing the subject. "Not when I'm baby-sitting the twins all the time."

"So you *do* think we've been asking you to baby-sit too much—I told Norman so," Mrs. Todd said as though she'd just solved a puzzle and won a prize.

"You guys don't have to talk about me behind my back all the time," Quinney said, starting to get angry again. "Why did you even have children anyway, if you can't stand us that much?"

She held her breath. She'd gone too far.

Mrs. Todd looked flabbergasted. "Quinney, we adore you!"

"Then how come you're always trying to get away from me?"

Mrs. Todd stood up and touched Quinney's arm. "We're *not* always—"

"Sure you are," Quinney scoffed, shaking off her mother's hand. "When you're not busy working, that is."

"That is just . . . not . . . true," Mrs. Todd announced in a shaky voice. "Would we be trying so hard to have another baby if that were true?"

"*What?*" Quinney yelped. "Another baby?"

"It's a secret, darling. I probably shouldn't have mentioned it," Mrs. Todd said.

"I can't believe it," Quinney said. Her lips felt numb.

Her mother looked puzzled. "What's so hard to believe?"

Quinney almost snorted, she was so angry. "You guys don't even take care of the kids you have! *I'm* the one who's always doing stuff, like—like folding laundry, and picking up toys, and fixing little snacks for the twins."

"Well, darling, nobody asks you to do those things," her mother said, trying to sound reasonable—but sounding a little annoyed instead.

Quinney goggled at her. "*Somebody* has to do them," she muttered.

"Why, Quinney? *Why* does someone have to?"

Mrs. Todd asked. "Do you think Teddy and Mack would starve if you didn't fix them snacks? No, they'd learn how to make their own messy little snacks. Do you think we'd all be running around naked if you didn't fold the clothes now and then? No, we'd just wear wrinkled clothes. It wouldn't be the end of the world."

"All the time. I fold the clothes all the *time*," Quinney said.

Mrs. Todd held up her hands. "You do it a lot, honey—I'll admit it. But don't you think maybe you *like* doing some of those chores? Doesn't it make you feel good to help?"

"Nobody likes picking up toys, Mom."

"Well, but you don't *have* to pick them up, Quinney. Walk on by when you see them lying there. Just say no!" Mrs. Todd said, smiling a little.

"That's not funny, *Mother*," Quinney said.

"Oh, darling—it's a *little* funny, isn't it?"

"No," Quinney almost growled. "Not even a little. Because," she said, her voice rising once more, "who wants to live in a pigsty? You guys just *can't* have another baby, Mom! I mean, where would you keep it?"

"Well, in the first place, Quinney, I'd hardly call our house a pigsty, even without your picking up after the boys. It's just *lived-in*, that's all."

"Lived-in," Quinney said, looking around their big old kitchen. Flowers that had been hastily arranged in jam jars dropped petals onto the table, three small red sneakers seemed to march along a countertop, and a wicker basket full of clean tangled underwear—with a Tonka truck on top—sat in front of the dryer. And now there was a tiny pyramid of sandwich crumbs on the kitchen table, crumbs that would probably still be there at dinnertime.

"And in the second place," Mrs. Todd continued, ignoring Quinney's meaningful stare around the room, "there's a lovely extra bedroom upstairs. It would be just perfect for a baby."

"*Mom!*" Quinney pleaded.

Mrs. Todd rearranged the salt and pepper shakers. "Well," she said, looking sad, "there's no point getting in an uproar, Quinney. It hasn't happened yet. It may never happen."

Quinney didn't know what to say. She turned away from her mother's unhappy face.

She tried to be fair as she thought about it. What if one of her listening customers asked her if she should have a baby? What if Ms. Ryder asked her?

Don't do it, Ms. Ryder! she would scream. *You're making a huge mistake!*

"What are you so worried about, darling?" her

mother asked in a gentle voice.

"It's hard to explain," Quinney murmured, tears filling her eyes. "It's kind of like—I don't know where I belong, exactly. In the family, I mean. And a new baby would just make everything worse."

Mrs. Todd gazed thoughtfully across the table at her daughter for a long moment, until Quinney grew even more uncomfortable than she already was.

"What?" Quinney asked. "What are you staring at?" She wiped at her eyes and shifted uneasily in her chair.

Her mother jumped a little, then laughed. "Oh, you know artists," she said. "I just suddenly had a mental picture of your daddy and me whirling around in a circle, perhaps even holding a new baby, and Teddy and Mack whirling around in another circle, and then there's poor little you, bouncing around all by yourself way off in the distance. I think that's how you must feel."

In the distance! "Thanks a lot!" Quinney exclaimed. "I'm not in the distance, I'm stuck right in the middle— like the top part of a wishbone," Quinney said, scrambling out of her chair. "And a new baby would just *snap* it, that's all!"

Her mother jumped up, too. "Quinney, darling, I'm sorry if what I said hurt your feelings. I guess I spoke without thinking, but I never meant that you—"

"I *am* all by myself, though," Quinney said, hot tears running down her cheeks at last. "You were right about that part, anyway."

"Sweetheart, no," Mrs. Todd said, distressed. "Never. You have us." She took a step forward, as if about to embrace her daughter, but hesitated when Quinney stepped back.

"Not now," Quinney said, her voice low. "Don't try to make everything all better, okay? Just let me be mad for a little while."

Mrs. Todd held up her hands as if in surrender. "It's a deal. Boy, you remind me of your father," she said. "And I mean that as a compliment," she added hastily. She fished a rubber band out of her skirt pocket and pulled her hair back, fastening it in a lumpy ponytail.

"I'm not anything like you *or* Daddy," Quinney burst out. "You must wonder where I even came from, sometimes. Well, maybe you'll have better luck with your next kid."

"Quinney, how can you say that?" Mrs. Todd said, shocked.

"It's obvious isn't it? Daddy's always trying to fix some broken-down old thing, or else he's dreaming about floating off down the river on a raft," Quinney said.

"And that doesn't sound even a little familiar, honey?" her mother asked, smiling now.

"I don't know *what* you are talking about," Quinney said haughtily.

"Well, think about it," her mother said, sounding reasonable. "Who else around here is always trying to come up with some logical system to make everyday life run a little smoother? Not to mention that *math* thing you guys do."

"I don't do that," Quinney lied.

"It's not such a bad thing, honey," her mother remarked.

"Hmm," Quinney said, suddenly not displeased at her mother's words. "And do you think I'm like you, too?" she asked shyly, after a moment.

Mrs. Todd nodded. "What about all that time you spend in your room with the door shut, Quinney?"

"I'm not mad at you guys or anything when I do that," Quinney said. "I guess I just need to be alone a lot."

Her mother nodded. "But part of you still wants to be with other people, right? With the family?"

"I guess," Quinney said.

"So where do you think that comes from, Quinney? Do you know anyone else like that?" Mrs. Todd was smiling now.

"I can think of one person," Quinney admitted, sneaking a look at her mom.

Mrs. Todd reached out a paint-stained finger and touched Quinney gently on the nose. "Look," she said, as if coming to a decision. "We'll talk more about this later, okay? But Quinney, I'm sorry you've been so upset lately. I mean, I knew something was troubling you, but I had no idea your feelings were this intense."

Quinney wiped her eyes with a little white T-shirt she'd grabbed from the laundry basket. "It's okay, Mom. And we don't have to have any more talks. But I'm sorry, I really *can't* baby-sit this afternoon. I'm sort of—well, I'm meeting someone at the library."

"Quinney!" her mom said, eyes sparkling. This exciting news made Mrs. Todd forget her baby-sitting request.

Oh, no, Quinney thought. She thinks I'm meeting a boy! Quinney would never hear the end of this one.

"Is it someone special, baby?" Mrs. Todd asked, grabbing another cookie.

"Mom, I'm only twelve!" Quinney said, laughing. Her mom was too much. "I'm the only girl I know who's getting dating pressure from her own *mother*. Anyway, it's nothing like that."

"Well, I certainly don't mean to pressure you, Quinney," Mrs. Todd said, holding up her hands.

"That's the last thing I'd do, you know that."

"I know," Quinney said. "But that's why I can't baby-sit. Sorry," she repeated.

Mrs. Todd shook her head. "That's okay," she said. "I'll think of something to keep them busy."

"Well, how about if I bring them home some books from the library? And read to them tonight?" Quinney said, wanting to help now.

"That would be great, honey," her mom said, smiling.

"Oh, Mom, I wanted to ask you. Uh . . . " Quinney's voice faded.

Go for it, she told herself. *Now's the time. Just say yes.*

"What, Quinney? You have a question for me?" Her mother's voice sounded hopeful.

"Well, I was just thinking, it's been a long time since we've all gone bowling, hasn't it? As a family?"

"Bowling?" Mrs. Todd said, as astonished as if Quinney had suggested that they all take up skydiving. "It sure has, baby. Like *never*. Can you really see Teddy and Mack at Bowl-A-Lot? Not to mention Monty! They're only five years old. It would be piping hot *chaos.*"

"We don't know for sure how old Monty is," Quinney teased. "And anyway, at least you wouldn't have to rent shoes for him."

"The boys are much too young for bowling," her mother said firmly. "But you're right, it *has* been a while since Norm and I have taken *you* bowling. And we could always get a sitter for the twins. I'll ask around."

"Well, I was hoping we could go tomorrow night," Quinney said. Marguerite would probably be there, she thought, helping her mom at the snack bar. Maybe she could corner her friend and talk to her.

And Cree might actually show up in person to warn Marguerite not to go to that party on Saturday. I just *have* to see what happens, Quinney thought, even if it does mean going on a date with my parents!

Her mom took another bite of cookie, starting to love the idea, but then her expression changed the same moment that the kitchen darkened. The storm was getting closer. "Oh, Quinney, I forgot—we can't. Not tomorrow, honey. The Sansoms are coming over for dinner."

Quinney thought fast. It *had* to be tomorrow, because the party was the night after that. "What about if I went to the bowling alley *alone* tomorrow night, to practice?" she said, desperate. "Then maybe the three of us could go together sometime next week."

"Well, I don't see why not," her mother said slowly.

"So I can go? Just for a couple of hours?"

"Yes—okay, it's settled," her mother said. "Will that make you happy, darling? One of us will drive you over, say at seven o'clock. Or eight?"

"Seven thirty, maybe," Quinney said, trying to choose the most logical time to arrive.

"Seven thirty, then. And then we'll pick you up at nine thirty sharp."

"Thanks, Mom," Quinney said, and she gave her mother an awkward hug. A flash of lightning lit up the darkened room, and a second later, thunder cracked and rumbled, seeming to shake the old house.

And Quinney suddenly thought, What if it starts to rain Saturday night during that stupid party? She pictured the steep dirt trails on Mahoney's Hill turning to slippery mud. *Or what if a bolt of lightning hits a tree on the hill? A tree that kids are huddling beneath?*

"Mom!" "Mommy!" the mingled voices of the twins cried out. Quinney heard their bare feet pounding down the stairs.

"Here we are," her mother called. Teddy and Mack burst into the kitchen, out of breath and with their hair mussed. "It's only thunder and lightning, sweeties."

"We know *that*," Mack said, scornful. "We weren't scared."

"We just heard you *chewing*," Teddy explained, as

he spotted the plate of cookies on the kitchen table.

"And swallowing," Mack added, with a look of reproach.

Ka-BOOM! A long crack of thunder shook the house again. As one, the twins jumped into their mother's lap.

Quinney laughed. "I'll pour some milk for everyone," she said. "I can see you guys are really hungry!"

Chapter Eleven

Five Good Things About Spike

An hour later, Mrs. Arbuckle was the only person in the library. Quinney waved hello, then quickly gathered up an armload of books for the twins, checked them out, and took her usual seat next to the dictionary.

Ms. Ryder was right on time.

"So, Quinney, did you get caught in the storm?" she asked.

"No, it stopped right before I left the house. Thank *goodness*."

"Me too. Well, enough chitchat," Ms. Ryder said, slapping a dollar bill onto the table. "Let's start talking."

"Did you make the list?" Quinney asked. "Five good things about your husband?"

Silently, the big woman fished in her purse, then slid a piece of paper face down across the table. Quinney turned it over:

Five Good Things About Spike (my husband).

1. He can be funny sometimes. Not as much as before, but still.

2. He is a good dancer. Except we hardly ever go out. Anywhere. I'm bored out of my skull.

3. He takes out the trash without me asking. But that's just once a week.

4. He is a good worker at work, he makes a good living.

5. He loves me. Even though we have nothing in common anymore.

"That's good," Quinney said, then wondered what to say next.

"It's good as far as it goes," Ms. Ryder said, frowning at the list. She looked up expectantly.

"Uh, let's look at these things one at a time, okay?" Quinney said, hoping that would take at least fifteen minutes.

"But that would use up the whole listening session," Ms. Ryder objected, as if she were reading Quinney's mind. "Maybe you could just kind of give me your overall impression?"

"You mean from the point of view of a twelve-year-old?" Quinney asked, desperate to make her aware of the goofiness of the entire situation.

"That's right," Ms. Ryder agreed. "From an objective point of view."

"Well, okay," Quinney said. "Um, first of all, I think I should tell you I spoke with your husband when I tried to call you."

"He told me," Ms. Ryder said, nodding. "He said, 'Some kid called,' then he gave me your message."

"Right. So the thing is, he sounded really, I don't know, *lonely*. Like he misses you."

"Yeah, he's lonely a lot," Ms. Ryder said, as though she were reporting the weather. "He hates it when I go out."

"You go out a lot?" Quinney asked.

Ms. Ryder nodded. "I like being around people. I see my friends, then there's meetings, and church, and church meetings. Not to mention going to the movies over in Peters Falls. But this professional listener stuff is the most fun I've had in a while," she added, beaming. "Dollar for dollar, especially."

I'm going to have to consider raising my rate, Quinney thought.

"Which reminds me," Ms. Ryder said, "Can I make another appointment for tomorrow? And Monday, and Tuesday? I'm assuming you take the weekends off."

"That's right," Quinney said.

Wow! Three more bucks, she thought, jubilant in spite of herself. This was working out great—if she could think of anything further to say to Ms. Ryder.

"But anyway, what is your general impression?" Ms. Ryder asked. "What did you think about my list?"

"Your husband sounds like a nice man," Quinney said truthfully.

"But like I said, *boring*," Ms. Ryder shot back. "He never wants to go anywhere. He says he's got me, and that's enough for him."

"Doesn't he see that if you guys get a divorce, he won't *have* you anymore?" Quinney asked.

"I haven't told him about the divorce yet. That I'm considering it, I mean."

"Was it going to be, like, a surprise? For Christmas?" Quinney asked, trying not to sound too sarcastic. Grown-ups were so weird.

Ms. Ryder scowled, her face redder than usual. "If Spikey *really* loved me, he'd know what I wanted."

"Well, unless he's Spike the Magnificent Mind Reader, I don't see how," Quinney said, nervous but determined.

"He's not a mind reader. He sells cars."

"Do you tell him about wanting to get out more?"

"No, I just go. By *myself*. He should have gotten the picture by now."

Quinney thought of her own mom and dad. Sometimes her mom told her dad, "I have to be alone for a while," or sometimes they both told Quinney and the twins, "*We* have to be alone for a while." But no one expected anyone else to automatically *know* what he or she wanted.

"So Quinney, what do you think? Should I get a divorce, or what?"

Oh, no, Quinney thought. There's that question again! Aloud, and trying to sound sure of herself, she said, "Okay, here's what I think. Remembering that I'm only twelve, and remembering that I'm supposed to be a listener, not an advice-giver—"

"Yeah, yeah," Ms. Ryder said, waving away these disclaimers, "but what do you *think*? My time's almost up!"

"Okay. I think—I think you should *not* get a divorce."

It was like flipping a coin, Quinney thought. Easy!

Ms. Ryder looked a little disappointed.

"But here's what I think you *should* do," Quinney went on quickly. "First, tell Spike you want to go out together at least once a week. At *least*. Maybe you should say twice a week. You guys could go for a walk, if money's a problem. But you have to start dating each other again," she added, thinking of her own parents.

"Well," Ms. Ryder said, "getting out twice a week together would be better than nothing, I guess."

"Wait a minute—I'm not done," Quinney said. "Second, you should tell him that you'll stay home alone with him at least that many times a week."

"*Doing nothing?*" Ms. Ryder objected, outraged in advance.

"No, not doing nothing," Quinney said, trying to remember the advice columns she now read regularly in the newspaper. "Plan something. Rent a video, or, um, cook a special dinner together, or play checkers or something. But make a plan. You guys can have a date, even at home! The point is, you each *give* a little."

"But what if that doesn't work?" Ms. Ryder asked.

"I think it *will* work," Quinney said. "Expect it to work, that's the key. Spike just sounds like the kind of guy who needs things spelled out for him. He's obviously no good at mind reading."

"You got that right," Ms. Ryder said with a grudging smile.

"But if you do all that, if you tell him what you want—and what you'll give—and he *still* won't make any changes, then you've really got a problem."

"And we can talk about it tomorrow? Another appointment?"

"I guess," Quinney said. They would finish at five, and there would still be plenty of time for her to get ready for her seven-thirty spy mission at Bowl-A-Lot.

"Well, also mark me in for Monday, Tuesday—and how about Wednesday?"

"Okay," Quinney said.

Pretty soon she'd have to increase her hours, she thought—just so she could fit in her other customers.

"So what's my homework for tomorrow?" Ms. Ryder asked eagerly.

"Your homework?"

"You know, like that list I made," Ms. Ryder said.

"Oh. Uh—well," Quinney said, her mind racing, "your homework is to think of two fun free things you and Spike could go out and do together, and then to tell him exactly what you want. Then think of two fun special things you could do together at home, too, and tell him *that* part of the plan."

"All that by tomorrow?"

"Yes, right," Quinney said, strict. She was relieved to see Mrs. Arbuckle bobbing toward them, straightening chairs and looking at her watch.

"It's a lot, but okay," Ms. Ryder said, getting up. She smiled suddenly at Quinney and added, "Boy, I really get my money's worth with you. I should tell all my friends!"

"Please don't," Quinney said weakly, but it was too late for Ms. Ryder to hear. She was already halfway to the door.

Chapter Twelve

Do I Know You from Somewhere?

"**W**ho remembers Aesop's story of the crow and the pitcher?" Quinney's father asked at breakfast early the next morning. Mrs. Todd was sleeping late, having worked in her studio until two A.M.

Quinney grinned at her father and buttered a piece of rye toast. She remembered this game of his fondly, even if she didn't play it anymore. Not often, at least.

Mack looked up at the ceiling, brown eyes thoughtful, but Teddy spoke first. "What's our prize for remembering?" he asked.

"The satisfaction of being an educated person," Norm Todd said, "*and* . . . this shiny new quarter!" He pulled a coin from his pants pocket.

"Do we lose money for wrong guesses?" Mack asked cautiously.

"No. And you each get one wrong guess," their father said.

"Um, is that the story where the crow won't let

anybody drink from the pitcher even though he's not thirsty?" Teddy guessed.

"Quinney? Is the first contestant correct?"

"I think he's getting the crow story mixed up with the dog in the manger story."

"Now I remember," Teddy said, excited. "That's where the dog won't let the donkeys eat hay, even though *he* can't eat it."

"That's right," his father said. "But what about—"

"The dog *could* eat the hay, though," Mack said, "if he was a vegetarian. So that fable's wrong. Maybe the dog was a vegetarian, and he was just hungry. Maybe those donkeys were trying to *steal* the hay."

Mack liked to consider every possibility.

"Ursop didn't say anything about the donkeys being stealers," Teddy objected.

"It's pronounced more like EE-Sop, son," his father corrected him.

"What about the crow and the pitcher?" Quinney reminded everyone, getting back to the original topic.

"Does the crow story have stones in it?" Mack asked.

"The crow story does, and the *pitcher* does," his father said, pleased.

"I remember, I remember," Mack said, excited. "See, there was this crow, and he was so thirsty!

And there was this pitcher with some water in it, but the crow couldn't reach the water. It was too far down."

"Oh yeah," Teddy said. "So he picked up a stone and dropped it into the pitcher—"

"No, *I'm* telling it," Mack said. "I'm the one who remembered."

"I think there's a quarter in this for each of you," their dad said, "but you guys have to finish telling the story first."

"So the water rose up a little when the crow dropped the stone in—"

"But he still couldn't drink, the water was too low—"

"So he dropped in another stone, and—"

"And another, and another, and—"

"And pretty soon the water was high enough for the crow to drink," Mack finished, triumphant.

Good old Dad! He hadn't lost the magic touch, Quinney thought.

"The water was all muddy," Teddy added, improvising, "but the crow didn't care."

"That's because mud's all right if you're a vegetarian," Mack pointed out.

Mr. Todd held up his hand for silence. "And what was Aesop's moral at the end of the story?"

"Is this part of the quarter, or is it a new contest?" practical Teddy asked.

"You guys remembered the story, so you already won your quarters," their father assured them. "But the moral's important, too."

"I can never remember the morals," Mack said, sounding sad.

"Me either," Teddy said. "I think they're the boringest part."

"Quinney? How about you? Do you remember the moral to the story of the crow and the pitcher?" her father asked.

"*Little by little does the trick,*" Quinney quoted.

"Whatever that means," Teddy said.

"She's right," her dad said, beaming. "That's my girl."

"I still think those morals are the boringest part of Ursop," Teddy said, "and so does Mack. And Monty thinks so, too."

Quinney reached her hand deep into the cold metal of her *Save-a-Cent* box again, hoping there would be another card there—one from Cree. Maybe it had gotten stuck.

But no, she was already holding the only two cards to arrive that morning.

One was from Toby:

Dear Qinny——Toby,

I hop you can come over to play, I haf a littel more time to play now. But I dont hav eny more money. But come over eny way.

Form your frend

Toby

Poor kid, Quinney thought. Maybe she'd stop by for a visit once she got the whole Marguerite disaster behind her, one way or another.

The other card was from Sam:

Dear Quincy,

Thanks for listening, I'll remember what you said. And thanks for telling me about that cleaning lady. She called and will be here on Friday, to clean and make dinner, too. I talked my ex-girlfriend Cynthia into coming over that night, she'll be impressed. I'll tell you about it at our appointment on Monday, hope that's a good day for you.

Sam

Monday! Quinney frowned. She could just see Sam and Ms. Ryder showing up at the library at the same time.

Well, she'd have to call one of them and cancel. Or maybe one customer could come fifteen minutes earlier. But could she count on that person to leave before the other one waltzed into the library? Which of them could she get rid of the easiest when the appointment was over? She stepped out onto the sidewalk.

"Tabby?" a voice interrupted her thoughts.

Oh, no, it's Mrs. Toby again, Quinney thought, quickly sliding Toby's postcard into her pocket.

"Hi," she said.

Mrs. Toby shifted her plastic grocery bag from one hand to the other. "Hello, dear," Mrs. Toby said. "I'm glad I bumped into you. I wanted to tell you that you got me thinking the other day."

"I did?"

Mrs. Toby nodded, solemn, and swatted a fly. "Yes, and I decided that maybe you're right. Maybe Toby's been working a little too hard on his lessons this summer. So we've been going out for nature walks together every afternoon. We're getting to know the neighborhood better."

"Oh, that's good," Quinney said. She didn't remember saying anything about nature walks.

"And the bonus is, we've met some nice children along the way. Well, Toby did. I stayed out of it pretty much. I just dawdled a little, to give him time to connect."

"That's good," Quinney said again. "Well, I have to—"

"So Toby has some new friends to play with, and I'm going to try to keep on staying out of it. Toby should be able to interact with his peers on his own."

"You mean he should play with other kids?" Quinney asked.

"Right," Mrs. Toby said with a laugh. "Play with other kids."

"Well, that's good," Quinney said once more, edging toward the door. "Tell him hi for me. And tell him I'll stop by for a little visit early next week if that's okay."

"I'm sure it is—if he's not busy *playing,* that is," Mrs. Toby added, winking.

"I'll take my chances," Quinney said. "Bye!"

The librarian was waiting for Quinney. "I think this is for you," she said, handing Quinney an envelope. "Ms. Ryder said to give it to the girl with the red hair."

"It's not really red," Quinney said, blushing, "but thanks, Mrs. Arbuckle."

"It's all right," the woman said, tucking a loose strand of her own decidedly gray hair behind one of her ears. "You seem to be very attached to the library," she added, sounding a little shy. "Are you interested in becoming a librarian some day, Mary?"

Mary! Nobody called Quinney that except for new teachers on the first day of school. But that was the name on her library card, Quinney remembered. "A librarian? I never really thought about it," she said.

"Well, maybe you should, dear. It can be a wonderful career, you know."

"Thanks. I'll keep it in mind," Quinney said.

Books, peace and quiet—it *did* sound pretty good, she admitted to herself as she took her seat next to the dictionary.

She looked down at the envelope in her hands. It had her name on it in round, loopy letters. She opened it as quietly as she could. There was a letter inside, and a worn dollar bill.

Dear Quinney,

I can't come today because your plan worked!

I am going out with Spike on a long walk. I guess I better cancel Monday, Tuesday, and Wednesday too, I just won't have room on my schedule. Spike says thanks a lot for trying to tie up all my time like that, but he probably doesn't mean it the way it sounds.

I just say thanks a lot, for everything! Besides, it was really fun. You know a lot for a kid. It was worth every penny.

Sincerely,

Ms. Ryder

Well, that was one customer down, Quinney thought, grinning. Success at this job would mean she was killing off her own business, little by little. At least she wouldn't have to cancel Sam on Monday.

Quinney blushed, though, thinking of Spike's remark about how she had been trying to tie up Ms. Ryder's time. And she was only trying to help!

She carefully folded the dollar and tucked it into her pocket, then she brightened. This cancellation gave her all the more time to get ready for tonight. And all the more time to feel nervous.

It was a perfect summer evening—a little warm, but not muggy. As Quinney's dad pulled up in front of Bowl-A-Lot, permanently stiff plastic flags seemed to wave jauntily from the building's painted stucco turrets. "Now, you have your money?" Mr. Todd asked.

"Yes," Quinney said, looking around. She squinted

at the neon castle in the window by the main door.

"And you've got your quarter for the phone call?" her father asked.

"Got it."

"No matter how much you spend, you're going to keep that quarter, right? To call home if you want to leave early?"

"Right, Dad. I promise," Quinney said. Her dad didn't have many rules, but he was strict about the ones he did have.

"And I'll check up on that quarter, don't think I won't. Now, you *promise* to call if you want to come home early, for any reason whatsoever. *I won't ask why.*"

Oh, no. He thinks I'm meeting a boy, too! Her mother had blabbed. Big surprise. "Thanks, Dad," Quinney repeated, opening the car door. She was afraid some high school kids would pull up behind them and honk. Or what if Cree came walking by and saw her sitting like a baby in her father's car?

"I'd better go," she said.

"Okay," her father said. "Well, one of us will pick you up at nine thirty, unless we hear from you before then. Oh, and don't forget to have fun! Save your scores for me."

"Bye, Dad," Quinney said gently.

Parents!

Popcorn and feet—that's what Quinney always thought of when she entered Bowl-A-Lot. In her opinion, Lake Geneva's Bowl-A-Lot was either the kind of place you liked to go when you were a little kid so you could run around like a nut while your parents bowled, or it was a place you went when you were a teen so you could hang out with your friends.

But when you were in-between, like she was, it was a place to avoid. She shuddered a little when she thought of bowling next week with her mom and dad. Marguerite owed her big for this one, even if she'd never know it.

Not that she was actually going to bowl tonight, Quinney thought. No, tonight was for spying! And if Cree didn't bother to show up, she would just have to warn Marguerite herself. Somehow.

The familiar clatter of falling pins mingled with shouts of laughter and tinny music as she made her way to the snack bar. When Marguerite was working, her specialty was nachos. She made nachos with salsa, nachos with jalapeños, and nachos with sour cream. But most of the time she sat cross-legged on a stool, watching everyone come and go.

"It's pathetic," she'd told Quinney once, but she went anyway. And she usually spent a long time getting ready to go, too, Quinney knew. She even put on makeup—lots of it.

Tonight, though, there was no sign of Marguerite. "Hi, Quinney," Marguerite's mom said, looking up from the Slushee machine. "Are your folks here tonight?"

"Hi, Mrs. Harper," Quinney said. "No, it's just me."

"You're here to bowl? I'm pretty sure you have to be with a group, Quinney, to get a lane on Friday night," Mrs. Harper said.

"I didn't know that. But it doesn't really matter. I'm not here to bowl. Did Marguerite ever get back from her aunt's house?"

"Oh, Quinney, yes, but she's not here. She's at home. She didn't want to come tonight—she said she was tired. She's not coming tomorrow either, she says. She's got *plans*," she said, mimicking her daughter. "Well, I guess everything changes," Mrs. Harper added, giving the speckled counter a quick swipe with her yellow sponge.

"Huh," Quinney said.

But she was thinking, Oh no! Now I'm stuck here for two whole hours. Because no way was she going to call her dad to come get her early. He probably wasn't even home yet.

What if Cree showed up, though? Where could she hide?

"Can I get you anything, Quinney? A snack or a soda?"

"No, thanks, I just ate." But this gave Quinney an idea. "Mrs. Harper? How about if I help you tonight for a while? It'd be good experience for me, and I think I could do it. I'm pretty sure I could fix the nachos, anyway."

"That'd be great, Quinney! You mean it?" Quinney nodded. Everyone who came to Bowl-A-Lot went over to the snack bar, sooner or later. If Cree showed up at all, she'd see him for sure.

And maybe he'd notice her. Maybe he'd think she was older than she was if he saw her working behind the counter. He wouldn't know *who* she was, but at least he'd know she existed.

And maybe she'd even think of something to say to him!

Right—like "hi," she thought, blushing.

"Well," Mrs. Harper said, "I'll be able to pay you a little something, hon. I know how you girls run through money. Now, wash up. I'll find a clean apron for you, and a cap."

Oh, great—now she'd look like a complete idiot. "Okay," Quinney said, and she pushed up her sleeves and started scrubbing her hands.

"I'm sorry Marguerite's not here tonight, honey," Mrs. Harper said, rearranging the sweating hot dogs as they rotated on the little stove's metal rollers. "I hope you're not too disappointed. Honestly, I don't know what has gotten into her lately. She's been so moody."

You think she's moody *now*, Quinney thought grimly, wait until Sunday morning, when she's in Intensive Care after her motorbike accident. . . .

People seemed to get hungry in waves, Quinney noticed. Things would be quiet at the snack bar for fifteen minutes, then all of a sudden there would be a line of people waiting. Quinney swirled bright orange melted cheese over chips in a loopy pattern, then sprinkled jalapeños on top, or spooned on salsa or sour cream. Some people requested all three toppings. "Think you can spare it?" one old man said when he thought she was being stingy with the cheese.

A couple of little kids who played with the twins recognized her. "Hi, Quinney," they said shyly, looking awed when she asked if she could help them.

Quinney only hoped that no one would tell her mom and dad about this.

* * *

"Excuse me, miss?" a familiar voice asked.

Quinney whirled around, dumping a spoonful of jalapeño discs onto the floor. It was Cree. She heard a buzzing in her ears and hoped she wouldn't faint right into the vat of hot orange cheese.

He's even cuter up close, Quinney thought.

Cree was wearing a baggy black cotton turtleneck and old khakis that were so faded they were almost white.

And he was still speaking: "Are you two the only people working here tonight?"

Mrs. Harper was busy making strawberry Slushees for a birthday party of eight-year-olds, so Quinney had to answer. She made her Bowl-A-Lot voice high and breathy, as different as possible from her professional listener voice. With any luck he wouldn't recognize it. "Uh, yes," she peeped, "we're the only ones here."

"Because I'm looking for a Margery, or Margaret, something like that," Cree said. "I heard she hangs out here sometimes."

I can't believe it—Cree Scovall actually took my advice! Quinney marveled to herself. It was all she could do not to laugh out loud. "Her name is Marguerite," she squeaked. "And usually she does work here, but not tonight. Can I take a message?"

Hey, she thought—this was working out perfectly! Apart from having to sound like Tweety-Bird, anyway.

Cree frowned, thinking. "No, I guess there's no message," he said finally. "It's kind of confidential," he added, smiling a little apology at Quinney.

"Well, I could give you her phone number, if you want," Quinney chirped. "I'm sure she wouldn't mind."

Mind? Marguerite would be forever grateful!

"Uh, no," Cree said, "I'd feel funny about calling. I don't even know her, not really," he added. "I just kind of wanted to tell her something." He ran his hand back through his acorn-brown hair, looking frustrated. "Well, I tried," he said, almost to himself.

"No, wait," Quinney called out in her normal voice, without thinking.

He couldn't just leave! What about Marguerite?

What about that awful party tomorrow night?

Cree turned to look at her, a question in his eyes. "Do I know you from somewhere?" he asked.

Quinney panicked. "No," she said, forcing her voice to go high again. "I don't think so."

He gave her a searching look. "I guess not," he finally agreed. Then he was gone, blending quickly into the noisy crowd.

"Hey," Mrs. Harper said, smiling at her, "wasn't that Cree Scovall? He is *cute*. Way to go, Quinney!"

"*Yeah, way to go,*" Quinney muttered, turning away. She was disgusted with herself.

Totally.

Chapter Thirteen

Marguerite

"Marguerite, it's me, Quinney." Quinney held the phone steady with her chin as she finished braiding her hair.

It was Saturday, the big day.

Quinney was all alone in the kitchen, for once. The twins were watching a video; her parents had decided to go back to bed.

Quinney looked out the window at a humid, hazy day and heard her friend yawn. I'm glad *somebody* got some sleep, she thought bitterly.

"Quinney, jeez. What time is it?"

"Nine thirty. I'm sorry, I thought you'd be up."

"So early?" Marguerite said, as though Quinney were crazy even to think it.

"I'm sorry I woke you," Quinney repeated.

"Well, I'm up now," Marguerite said grouchily. "What do you want, anyway?"

"I—I just wanted to talk about some stuff,"

Quinney said. "I hardly saw you at all last week."

"You know I had to go stay with my aunt," Marguerite said. "And then I was shopping for the party tonight and everything," she added, lowering her voice. "You should see what I got!" she added, cheering up.

"Well, what about today?" Quinney asked. "You could show me what you got. And anyway, I have to talk to you."

"About Cree Scovall, right?" Marguerite's voice was suddenly teasing. "Mom told me all about it last night when she got in."

"She told you *what*?"

"That Cree Scovall was talking to you at the snack bar. Your dream come true," Marguerite added.

Quinney could almost see her friend rolling her eyes. "He was talking about *you*, Marguerite," she said, embarrassed—and a little angry. She kicked at a small hooked rug her mother had picked up at a tag sale.

"Me?" Marguerite's voice dropped to a whisper. "You're kidding."

"No, I'm not kidding," Quinney snapped.

"What did he say?"

"Look, I'd really rather have this conversation in person. Can't I just come over?"

"Sure!" Marguerite sounded wide awake now. She

giggled. "See, Quinney, I *told* you that you should have gone with me to that party last weekend. Because Cree was one of the guys who was there!"

Quinney was flushed and sticky by the time she reached Marguerite's house, only three blocks away. It was going to be a nasty day. Insects chirped frantically in the morning heat, and small dusty birds rolled in dew-soaked grass, desperate for a bath.

Marguerite was waiting on the screened-in front porch. Its screens were so old and dark that Quinney could barely see her friend from the sidewalk. Marguerite looked like a giant exotic moth pressed against them.

She was still in her nightgown, and the aqua nylon hung limp in the damp air. "Come on back to my room," she whispered to Quinney. "Mom's still asleep, and anyway, I don't want her to hear this."

"What about your father?" Quinney whispered back. "Where's he?"

"He moved out for a few days, but he'll be back," Marguerite said in her don't-ask-me-any-more-questions voice.

The two girls settled in on Marguerite's unmade bed, and Quinney looked around. Marguerite's room was much like her own except that Marguerite was a lot messier, and she had a dressing table. The dressing table was the neatest spot in the room. Its mirrored surface was cracked and half-covered with cosmetics and little nail polish bottles, arranged by shade: corals, pinks, reds.

Marguerite's acting like she's in high school already, Quinney thought scornfully, looking at the table. But she wished she could examine the blushers and eyelining pencils more closely.

"Well?" Marguerite asked.

"Oh, yeah," Quinney said, reluctant to begin.

"So come on, what did Cree say about me? Tell!"

"First, he asked if you were at the bowling alley."

"Oh, I *knew* I should have gone. I almost went, but Friday nights are usually so lame. Just families and old people," Marguerite said.

"*Anyway,*" Quinney continued, "I said no, you weren't there, but I told him that I could give you a message if he wanted. But he said no."

"It was probably something personal he wanted to say," Marguerite said. She hugged her knees to her chest, pleased, and ran her hands lightly up and down her shins.

She was shaving her legs already, Quinney realized, startled.

"Go on," Marguerite urged.

"Yeah, it was probably personal," Quinney said, glum. "So then I said I could give him your phone number."

"Quinney! You're brilliant." Marguerite's eyes shone with excitement.

"But he said no to that, too," Quinney said quickly.

"He *did*? You mean, he didn't want my phone number?" Marguerite looked stricken.

"He said he'd feel funny about calling, since he didn't really know you."

"He knows me a little," Marguerite said, perking up. "Enough to come looking for me, anyway."

"Yeah," Quinney said. "Well, then he said he just had something to tell you. And then he left."

Marguerite leaned forward. "He said he had something to tell me?" she repeated.

"And he looked worried," Quinney added, exaggerating.

How on earth could she warn Marguerite not to go to that party tonight, without betraying Cree?

Now, Marguerite looked worried too, as if in sympathy. "Worried? Like how?" she asked.

"Oh, I don't know," Quinney said, feeling helpless. "What *happened* at that party last Saturday, anyway?" she asked. "You never said."

"Oh, it was so great, Quinney—all these kids were

there," Marguerite gushed. "Older kids, I mean—not babies. I wore my black jeans, my boots, and this top—well, you should see it. Wait, I'll show you!"

Marguerite leaped off the bed and ran to her bureau. She opened the bottom drawer and rummaged under some sweaters.

When she stood up, she was holding something that looked like a lacy black scarf. "Look!" Marguerite said, draping it against her chest. "You can't tell now, but it looks really good on," she added.

"It's a tube top?" Quinney guessed.

"A tube top," Marguerite confirmed, nodding. "There's spandex in it so it doesn't fall down," she added, with a smirk. She tossed the garment to Quinney.

"Huh," Quinney said, catching it. She gave the tube top an experimental tug. All the spandex in the world couldn't hold this thing up on me, she thought, glancing ruefully at her own flat chest.

"And I wore tons of makeup—I probably looked sixteen, at least," Marguerite babbled on. "And it worked!"

"Worked like how?"

"Well, for one thing, nobody said anything about me showing up there. And there were these guys! Not just Cree," she added, giggling. "Anyway," she continued, "these other guys were just standing around, laughing and stuff. One of them was really cute, so I just made myself walk right up to him and start talking. And after that it was easy."

"It was?"

"Yeah. I could tell he was interested in me. The other guys were, too. It was so cool—they were asking me all these questions, like where I went to school and stuff. They thought maybe I was just here for the summer." Marguerite giggled again. "You know, a rich kid from Snob Hill," she explained, naming the area a couple of miles out of town where the biggest, oldest houses in the area stood.

"Then what happened?" Quinney asked, fascinated in spite of herself.

"So I was being all mysterious and stuff, and it was so great, but then I figured I'd better leave before I wrecked it somehow. You know, like in 'Cinderella'! This guy was practically begging me for my phone number by then, and his friends were all teasing him because I wouldn't give it to him. But I promised him I'd be at the next party. He made me promise, practically!"

"He did?"

Marguerite nodded. "And that's tonight. But I didn't know Cree Scovall had noticed me too! *Cree Scovall*. I'd much rather have him. I wonder if I can ditch that other guy. . . ."

Quinney took a deep breath. "I think maybe this whole party thing is a big mistake," she interrupted. She hated hearing Marguerite talk about Cree like this—as if he was a prize for her to win.

"A mistake? Like how?" Marguerite asked, her voice suddenly frosty.

"Well, like maybe you shouldn't go back there tonight. These kids are a lot older than you, and it's going to be dark and everything. It might start raining, even."

"Ooh, scare me to death, Quinney—it'll be dark! Maybe that's because it will be *night*," Marguerite said, sarcastic. "That's when all the fun happens, in case you haven't noticed. Anyway, a little rain never hurt anyone. You're getting to be worse than Brynn, and that's saying something."

Quinney took another deep breath and tried again. "There's nothing wrong with Brynn. But Marguerite, look—"

"No, *you* look, Quinney," Marguerite interrupted. "You're jealous! I know you like Cree Scovall, and here he finally comes walking up to you last night—but when he does, he's looking for *me*. I'm sorry if that hurt your feelings, but tough! I can't control it if boys like me."

"I'm not jealous," Quinney said, knowing that wasn't exactly the truth.

"Oh, sure," Marguerite said. "Look, Quinney, it's like my mom says. Some girls just mature faster than others."

She stretched—emphasizing her boobs, Quinney thought, turning to look out the window. "You're only twelve," she said, staring hard at a tree. "Just like me and Brynn."

"But I'm a *mature* twelve," Marguerite said. "Brynn is like twelve going on nine. And you—oh, you're all sensible and stuff. Anybody has any questions, they just ask Quinney! And you have all the answers, right? But I'm not talking about that. I'm talking about being *physically* mature." Marguerite smoothed her nightgown against her legs in a self-satisfied way that infuriated Quinney. "And obviously, that's something guys like," Marguerite added, smiling a little.

Quinney jumped up, angry. "Marguerite, you can be so—so *dense*," she sputtered.

"And you can be so childish," Marguerite said, her voice smug. "Look, Quinney, I'm sorry if this is bothering you, but what I said is the truth. And it's a *fact* that Cree Scovall was interested in me, not in you."

"Marguerite—"

"Look, I'm not even going to *ask* you to go with me tonight. Not anymore! You had your chance, and obviously you're just not ready yet for a mature relationship."

"Well, neither are you!"

"That's not up to you to decide," Marguerite said, smiling in an annoying way. "Now, you'd better go home. I have a lot of stuff to do before tonight."

"I'm already gone," Quinney said, her voice shaking. "And Marguerite—you *deserve* whatever happens to you!"

The *nerve* of her, Quinney thought as she stormed home, calling me jealous, when I was only trying to help. Well, *let* Marguerite go to that party tonight. I did everything I could.

Quinney tried to push the whole thing out of her mind. Who cared what happened to Marguerite, anyway? Maybe it would serve her right—teach her a lesson, like that guy said. She could barely believe they'd ever been friends.

They had nothing in common. *Nothing.*

"Quinney!"

Quinney stopped in the middle of the sidewalk, surprised at hearing her name. Brynn had pulled her bike up right next to her and was waiting for a response. "Oh, hi Brynnie," Quinney said. "I didn't see you."

"Gee, how could you miss me?" Brynn asked, laughing, as she glanced down at her hot-pink T-shirt. Then she looked searchingly at Quinney and asked,

"Hey, is something the matter?"

Quinney bit her lip to keep from answering her too fast. She knew what she *wanted* to say. And she knew that Brynn would listen and agree with her that Marguerite had really gone too far this time. But she'd probably say that no matter what had happened. So why even tell her?

Brynn had made it clear how she felt about Marguerite, and now Marguerite had made it clear how she felt about Brynn, too. And I'm in the middle again, Quinney thought.

Who was she supposed to talk to now?

No, blabbing to Brynn wouldn't help anything, Quinney thought. "Nothing's the matter," she said. "I'm just in a hurry to get home, that's all. I'll call you later, okay?"

"Okay," Brynn said, but Quinney was halfway down the block.

Chapter Fourteen

Mr. Todd

"Quinney-Quin-Quin," her father said as soon as she walked in the door. "Can we talk for a minute?"

"I guess," Quinney said.

Uh-oh, she thought. This meant trouble—her dad didn't usually seek her out this way. But she wasn't in the mood for her family right now—she had enough problems today.

He was finally ready to talk to her about the fight she'd had with her mom, Quinney realized suddenly. Her father did that—he waited for a problem to *digest*, as he put it, before he felt comfortable analyzing it.

Oh, why did her parents have to go and tell each other *everything*? Now her dad was going to scold her—and maybe talk about the stupid baby. That *maybe-baby*.

And there was no way she could get out of it.

Mr. Todd brushed off a sofa cushion with a flourish.

He held his freckled hand out as if he were seating Quinney at a restaurant. The blond hair on his forearms glinted in the sunlight.

"Thanks, Daddy," Quinney said, feeling foolish. "What's up?"

Her father hitched his pants up, sat down, turned to face his daughter, and cleared his throat. He ran his hand back through his reddish hair. In spite of working with kids all day long during the school year, he looked uncomfortable here, now, with his own daughter.

"Well," he began, "your mother and I were talking last night, and she told me a little of what's been troubling you."

"It's no big deal," Quinney said. She made a slight movement as if getting up to go, but her father put his hand on her arm.

"It's a big deal if it's something that's really bothering you, Quin."

Quinney shrugged his hand away and crossed her arms, suddenly not knowing what else to do with them. "I don't mind baby-sitting," she finally said. "It's just that I had something else to do that day."

"I think there was more to it than that," Mr. Todd said.

Quinney simply didn't want to talk. "Look, do you want me to apologize? Because I will, if that's what you want," Quinney said. "But I don't see why this can't just be between me and Mom."

"We're a team, Quinney," her father said patiently. His patience only made her madder, though.

"You sure are," she muttered.

There was silence for a moment, and then Mr. Todd tried another approach. "Your mom told me you suggested that we *all* go bowling some time. And so we got to thinking last night that we should all do more together, as a family. You know, family activities," he added carefully, as if pronouncing a foreign phrase.

"But Daddy, we're too busy for family activities," Quinney objected. Oh, why had she ever complained to her mother? Now look!

"Too busy?" Mr. Todd blinked, surprised.

"Well," Quinney pointed out, "you have your hobbies, and Mom has her art, and the twins have each other." She decided not to mention the maybe-baby.

"And what about you, Quinney?" her father asked. "What do you have?"

"Oh, I supervise all you guys, and my friends, too," Quinney said, trying a joke. "I guess that's my job— even though I'm not doing so great with my friends lately."

"Why?" Mr. Todd asked. "What's going on with your friends? Maybe I can help."

"Nobody can help," Quinney said glumly. "It's just that Brynnie and Marguerite don't really like each other so much anymore. And now Marguerite and I have had a fight."

"Mmm," Mr. Todd said thoughtfully.

So *he* had learned the listening noise too, Quinney thought, and she smiled in spite of herself.

"What happened?" her father asked.

"Well, Marguerite is about to make this huge mistake," Quinney said in a rush. "*Please* don't ask me for any details, okay? But I tried to warn her about it, and she basically told me to mind my own business. In a really mean way, too!"

Quinney's father frowned. "What kind of mistake is Marguerite about to make?" he asked.

"Oh, don't worry—she's not going to rob a bank or anything," Quinney said, trying another joke. She stared down at the rug. "It's nothing like that, but I'm still worried. I can't help it. So anyway," she added, trying to keep things light, "I guess that means I'll have to concentrate on supervising you guys."

"Well," Mr. Todd said slowly, "we *have* been relying on you a lot, Quinney. It seems as though everything just came together at once, this summer—your mom's show, and you being so mature all of a sudden and having all this free time, and so on."

You think I'm mature, Quinney thought. You should tell that to my body. You should tell that to Marguerite!

"Plus," her father continued, "we've been feeling—well, a little more romantic lately, and—"

"It's okay," Quinney interrupted. "You don't have to tell me that."

"But on weekends, at least," he continued, "we decided that we should be doing more things together as a family."

"Why bother?" Quinney grumbled. "You know you guys would rather be alone!"

"*What?*" her father exclaimed.

"I said—you'd rather be alone," Quinney repeated, blushing now. "Oh, come on, Dad! It's the truth, isn't it? I'm surprised you guys even had kids!" She still thought this, despite what her mother had said.

Her father didn't speak for a minute or two—so long that it was all Quinney could do to keep from looking at her watch. Then, to her surprise, he smiled a little. "Did I ever tell you how I got started on Mark Twain?" he asked.

Mark Twain? Quinney shook her head, silent.

"It was right after you were born, Quinney," her father began. "We'd been wanting a baby for a long time, but . . . it's not always so easy to have one," he said, faltering.

Quinney's heart was pounding. "You're not about to tell me that I'm adopted, are you?" she asked. Although that would explain a lot, she thought.

Mr. Todd laughed. "No," he said. "I was just trying to explain the way people get to feeling when they really want to have a baby, but they can't."

"But I don't get it," Quinney said. "You had me, didn't you?"

"After five years," her father said, looking down at his big hands. "It took five years, Quinney."

"I never knew that," Quinney said. "I mean, I knew that you guys had been married for five years before I came along, but—well, I just figured you were out having fun that whole time."

"Well, not every single minute!" her father said, smiling.

Quinney thought for a moment. "But what does that have to do with Mark Twain?" she finally asked.

"Ah!" her father said, his eyes shining at the memory. "Let's see," he said. "How did it happen, exactly? I think I must have picked up a magazine just before you were born, when your mother and I were down in Saratoga Springs seeing the doctor. And it happened to have an excerpt from *Roughing It,* one of Twain's earlier works."

"I never heard of that one," Quinney said.

"He wrote it when he went out West, before he had a family of his own," Mr. Todd said.

"So it's real?" Quinney asked.

"Well, you know Twain—a lot of it's real, but some of it he probably made up. Who knows? But the point is, this excerpt included a story about a miner he heard about who came into San Francisco during the gold rush days."

"Mmm," Quinney said.

"During the time he was writing about," Mr. Todd said, sounding more and more like a teacher with each word, "San Francisco was a pretty rough place, and there were hardly any women or children there. And all the men got terribly homesick for them."

"Mmm," Quinney said.

"So the story went that this new family had arrived by ship, and they were just disembarking with their two-year-old daughter when a fierce old miner spotted them. He had just come down from the mountains, and when he saw the little girl he was so moved that he offered a sack of gold dust just to kiss her."

"A sack of gold dust?"

Mr. Todd nodded. "Worth a hundred and fifty dollars. And that was *then*, Quinney. It would be worth a whole lot more now. We could figure it out!" he added enthusiastically.

"Maybe later," Quinney said.

"Anyway," her father continued, settling back into his tale, "the thing is, I just about fell apart when I read that article—because I knew exactly how that old miner felt!"

"You did?" Quinney asked.

"Yep. I felt that way whenever I thought about you, Quin."

"Even before I was born?" Quinney asked, shy and pleased.

Her father nodded again. "And you started moving around inside your mom just as I finished the article, and she asked me if I wanted to feel you kick. I told her yes, it was worth at least a sack of gold dust to me." He cleared his throat.

Quinney stared at the blurry rug under her feet.

"And so that's how I got started on Mark Twain," Mr. Todd announced.

"Huh," Quinney said, blinking hard.

"Children are good news," her father added in a quiet voice.

Quinney listened to herself breathe for a moment.

"But now you've got me kind of worried about Marguerite," Mr. Todd said, trying to change the subject. "Isn't there *anything* I can do?"

Quinney shook her head. "I talked and talked to

her, Dad," she said wearily. Rage at her friend had made her tired, she discovered.

"And there's nothing else you could try?" he asked. "Nothing?"

"Nope. Except—well, maybe there's one thing," Quinney said, as the idea formed.

She *did* still have Cree Scovall's phone number. . . .

Chapter Fifteen

No Problem

It took all her courage to telephone. "Hello, is um, your son there?"

"No, he's out. Sorry. Who is this, please?"

Now what? "Oh, it's—it's—"

"No, wait a minute, he just walked in the door. Cree, it's the phone, for you."

Quinney almost slammed down the receiver, but she restrained herself. "Hello?" She could barely hear Cree's voice over the roaring in her ears. Why did he always seem to have this effect on her?

"Uh, C?" she said, pitching her voice grown-up, low. "This is the professional listener."

"Oh," he said, startled, "just a minute." There was the muffled sound of a door closing. "Okay, I'm back," he said.

"I'm sorry to bother you like this."

"It's okay, I was just surprised, that's all."

"Well, I wouldn't have called, except I—I sort of

stumbled across a phone number I thought you might like to have."

"A phone number? What phone number? Whose?"

"It's that girl's, the one you wanted to warn about the party tonight. Her name's Marguerite, by the way."

"Yeah, that's the one," he said. "But how did *you* find out her name? And her phone number?"

"I have a lot of connections," Quinney said, vague. "So do you want the number or not?"

"I guess so, sure. Let me get a pencil." Quinney heard a sticky drawer squeak open, then he was back. "Okay," he said.

There was still time to hang up, Quinney told herself. But no. "It's 7228," she told him. "Oh, and C?"

"Yeah?"

"Don't say who you got her number from, okay?"

Cree laughed. "No problem," he said. "It's not like it's something I'd mention—and I don't even know who you are. I still think this whole listening thing is pretty weird. No offense, ma'am."

Cree Scovall had called her *ma'am*!

Quinney wanted to curl up and die.

Chapter Sixteen

Sunday

Sunday mornings always meant pancakes and bacon at Quinney's house. Mr. Todd cooked, Quinney, Teddy, and Mack helped, and Mrs. Todd got to stay in bed late.

Quinney couldn't stop yawning as she poured the maple syrup—the specialty of a nearby farm—into its pitcher. She'd thought she would never fall asleep last night, wondering whether or not Cree had really called Marguerite.

Or had he given up trying? Had Marguerite gone to that party on Mahoney's Hill?

Teddy called Mrs. Todd to the table and they all sat down, still in their pajamas and bathrobes. "Pass the butter, please," Mack said.

"Here it is," Quinney said, handing it to him as she hid another yawn.

"*Merci,*" Mack said.

"Wait a minute," Quinney said, waking up fast.

"Hold on. Since when do you speak French?"

"Since yesterday. Right, Teddy?"

"*Bonjour.* We know lots of French," Teddy agreed.

"So we should probably be eating French toast!" Mack snickered his approval of this joke.

"But how did you—hey, *wait* a minute," she repeated. "Do you guys know a kid named Toby?"

"He's our new best friend," Mack said. "Besides Monty, that is."

"But Toby *likes* Monty," Teddy reassured them all.

"Who wouldn't?" Quinney's dad asked. "What's not to like?"

"Quinney, how do *you* know Toby?" Mrs. Todd asked sleepily, cradling her coffee cup.

"Oh, just from walking around town," Quinney said.

"Well, you should have introduced him to the twins," she said. "He was one lonely little guy."

"I didn't think they'd like each other." She turned to her brothers, whose faces were sticky with syrup. "I mean, Toby's older, and everything."

"Not that much older," her mother pointed out. "Anyway, Toby and his mother were out walking the other day, and they spotted Teddy and Mack under a tree, communing with nature."

"No," Teddy corrected her, "we were talking with

Monty. And we saw them first."

"Well, the point is, you kids had fun together," she told him. "The twins were invited over there to play yesterday afternoon," she added for Quinney's benefit.

Quinney was amazed. "They were? Where was I?"

"I don't know," her mother said, puzzled. "Up in your room, probably. Why?"

"I'm just surprised, that's all," Quinney said. "What did you guys do over there?" she asked her brothers.

"Nothing. We just *played*," Teddy said.

"Don't tell her," Mack whispered to him. "It's none of her business. Besides, she's a girl."

"Toby is coming over here to spend the night," her father told her, "so you can see them play with your own two eyes, honey."

"*I'm* not going to play with her two eyes," Teddy informed his giggling twin.

"Toby's coming *here*?" Quinney asked. "When?" Her mind raced. Would her secret finally be revealed?

"Tomorrow night."

"If it's not raining, we can sleep outside, maybe. In sleeping bags!" Teddy said, sputtering pancake.

"Or in the living room," Mack said, more cautious.

"But what about Toby's mom?" Quinney asked. "I mean, I got the impression she was a little protective. Just from what I heard, I mean."

"His mom can't come," Teddy said firmly. "It's boys only. No ladies. Not even you, Quinney."

"Quinney's not a lady, Monty says," Mack contributed. "But she can't come anyway."

"Toby's mother was a little surprised at the invitation," Mrs. Todd said, "but Toby really wanted to come, so she finally said okay. We can always take him home if it doesn't work out."

"It'll work out," Mack said. "Hey, Quinney," he added, eyeing her plate, "are you going to eat your bacon? Because Monty *loves* bacon."

"Here, Monty," Quinney said, holding out the crispy strip.

"She's in *shock*," Teddy whispered to his brother. "Quick, take it!"

"Quinney, telephone for you," her mother called up the stairs early that afternoon. "It's Marguerite."

Marguerite! Well, at least she was still alive. "Just a second," Quinney said. She rushed into the guest room and picked up the phone. "Marguerite?"

"Hi, Quin! It's me," Marguerite said in her are-you-still-mad-at-me voice.

"I know," Quinney said. "Are you all right?" she asked.

"Of course I'm all right," Marguerite said. "I'm

better than all right! Quinney, look—I'm really sorry about yesterday, about those things I said. I just wanted to tell you that."

"Okay, thanks. Now you've told me," Quinney said.

"No, I really mean it," Marguerite said. "You were right about staying home from that party last night."

"You stayed *home*?" Quinney could scarcely believe what she was hearing.

"Yeah—the most incredible thing happened, you'll never guess," Marguerite said. *"Cree Scovall* called me. Yesterday afternoon!"

"He did?" Quinney said. She gripped the telephone receiver and was flooded with different feelings. Relief, jealousy—and even a little pride that her plan had worked.

"He must have really wanted to talk to me," Marguerite said, as if thinking aloud, "to go to all that trouble to get my number. Don't you think?"

"I guess," Quinney said. "So what'd he say?"

"Oh, a bunch of stuff. You know, like he talked about that party last weekend. It's not that interesting," Marguerite said. It was obvious that she didn't want to go into detail.

He had told her about that guy and what he was going to do to her, Quinney guessed.

"But the main thing," Marguerite went on quickly, "is that after he said all that, he told me he'd gone looking for me at Bowl-A-Lot, and I said I was usually there on weekends. So Quinney, you'll never guess!"

"What?" Quinney said, glum.

"Well, he asked if I was going there *that* night. You know, last night. So of course I said yes, I was going to be there, because I could tell he wanted me to. And I went, and Quinney—you'll never guess!"

Marguerite should start a new game show called *You'll Never Guess*, Quinney thought bitterly.

"Quinney?"

"I'm still here."

"You're so quiet," Marguerite said. "Anyway, so he came to Bowl-A-Lot last night. Cree Scovall! And I fixed him these great nachos, you should have *seen* them, and he kept hanging around."

"Mmm," Quinney said, making her listening noise.

"So my mom told us to go bowl, but we didn't want to. So we played some of those lame old pinball machines, and it was *so much fun*. I'm sorry Quinney— I know you sort of like Cree, but I really think he likes me."

Maybe he did, Quinney thought gloomily. "And what about you, do you like him?" she asked Marguerite.

"Quinney, he's *Cree Scovall*. Of *course* I like him! Can you imagine how cool it will be when we start school? Here I'll be, this sixth-grade kid, and the most famous guy in eighth grade already *likes* me?"

"That'll be great," Quinney said, miserable.

"Oh, and he's coming over here, to my house, tomorrow night. Mom will be home, but that's okay."

"That's great, Marguerite," Quinney repeated dully.

"So . . . I just wanted to tell you what happened."

"It's lucky he called you when he did," Quinney said, thinking of the part she'd played in making that call possible. She was tempted to tell Marguerite all about it, or just enough to impress her—and to bring her back down to earth.

But she couldn't.

"Luck!" Marguerite sounded surprised. "Quinney, if I hadn't gone to that party on the hill in the first place, I never would have flirted with those guys. And if I'd never flirted with those guys, Cree never would have noticed me. And if he had never noticed me, he never would have gone to all that trouble to find out who I was and get my phone number! That's the moral here: You have to take chances. See how it works?"

"Yeah, I see." She's clueless, Quinney thought.

She saw how people believe what they wanted to, anyway.

"You have to take chances, Quinney," Marguerite repeated solemnly as though she were quoting her new motto. "But I really am sorry for saying how immature you are. It's not true. Brynnie, maybe, but not you. Hey, Cree even asked me who that girl was at the snack bar on Friday night. You really made an impression! He kept saying he thought he knew you from someplace."

"Well, he doesn't," Quinney said flatly. *And he never will, either,* she added to herself.

Not now.

Chapter Seventeen

Now What?

Ma'am!

Cree Scovall's voice still seemed to echo in Quinney's ears as she walked over to the tiny *Save-a-Cent* office early Monday morning. There were four postcards in her box, but she didn't even look at them. Instead she sighed, stuffed them into her shorts pocket, and headed toward home.

She decided to take the route that passed the little park by the creek that she, Brynnie, and Marguerite liked best. Well, those days were gone forever, she thought. Why did things—and *people*—have to change? Quinney flopped down on the grass.

Ma'am.

Oh, why had she ever thought she could be a professional listener? Giving advice and having all the answers—what a joke!

Quinney rolled over onto her stomach. She scowled and poked at the ground with a stick while she thought of the mess her own life was in.

For example, Brynn and Marguerite were barely speaking and there was nothing she could do about it. And then Marguerite was convinced that she, Quinney, was jealous of her, so obviously *their* friendship would never be the same.

On top of everything else, Quinney thought gloomily, she'd never get to know Cree Scovall now.

This is all my parents' fault, Quinney thought suddenly, squinting her eyes as she rolled over onto her back and looked up at the brilliant leaves as zillions of tiny gnats flew around above her head. Her parents! She wouldn't be the stupid way she was, telling everyone else what to do, if her mom and dad weren't the way *they* were—always wrapped up with each other.

The more Quinney thought about it, the more sense it made.

They had almost *forced* Quinney to be a professional listener!

Oh, what her mother had said made a little sense, too, Quinney admitted to herself grudgingly. She didn't *have* to pick up after the twins all the time. They would just grow up to be slobs if she kept on doing that.

Huh, Quinney thought. That's all we need.

But if maybe-baby really came along—well, Quinney

didn't want to think about that! The house would just be—how did her mother put it? *Piping hot chaos,* Quinney remembered with satisfaction.

There was nothing she could do about the baby, though, Quinney realized, almost with relief. In fact, there were lots of things she couldn't do anything about.

But where did knowing all that leave her *now*? Should she give up and go out of the listening business? Quinney threw her arms over her head in frustration.

Something crinkled, and she remembered the post-cards in her pocket. She fished them out and read the first one.

Dear Professional Listener,

I need help fast. My father's dog Marshmallow is about to have puppies and my mother says no way can we keep even one. She's even mad at Marshmallow and it's not her fault she got pregnant. I'm afraid my mom will take them all to the pound, and I mean Marshmallow too. Please call me, my number is 1332.

Sincerely,

Charlotte

Oh my gosh, Quinney thought. Poor dogs. Poor Charlotte, whoever she was.

Dear listener,

    I know you said no medical advice, but this isn't really medical, not exactly. Here is what I want to talk about: I'm too short for my age, and it's making my life miserable. I know you can't make me grow, but maybe you could at least listen. My mom won't help me, she says I'm perfect the way I am. My dad says I'll grow some day. But what if he's wrong? Anyway, he's short too.

    My phone number is 4163.

    From

    Mark

    p.s. I'm nine

Only nine, Quinney thought. Poor kid.

Dear Quinney,

    I'm sorry for what I said on the phone. I was wrong to blame you for anything. I should have thanked you instead, because now my wife and I are starting to have more fun together. I have to take her out on dates again, but she stays home more too. We even started a darts tournament last night.

    Sincerely,

    Spike Ryder (Ms. Ryder's husband)

Darts, Quinney thought, alarmed. She would have suggested something a little less—less *lethal*.

Dear Professional Listener,

I am almost thirteen and very mature for my age.

My problem is my best friend. We had this fight today. I got mad and told her she was jealous of me, but I'm more jealous of her sometimes! She has this perfect family. I love my mom and dad but they're not perfect. And I'm afraid they're splitting up! But anyway, I don't know how to say I'm sorry to my friend. The words keep coming out wrong when I practice. So maybe if I talked with you it would help. I have the dollar, it would certainly be worth it. My number is 7228.

Marguerite

Marguerite! Marguerite is jealous of *me*, Quinney thought, flabbergasted. She never would have guessed it.

And Marguerite still wanted to be friends!

But how could she think Quinney's weird family was perfect? It wasn't. Nobody's family was perfect, Quinney thought.

She shuffled through the four postcards again, frowning a little. What should she do with them? Obviously, she owed these people something—well, Charlotte and Mark, anyway. Just those two kids, and then she would quit. She should call Charlotte and Mark right away, this very night, Quinney told herself.

She should probably tell them, "Sorry, I've gone out of the listening business for good." But then who would they talk to? Maybe they didn't have anyone else.

It must be so hard for Mark, being smaller than all the other kids.

And what about Marshmallow? And those puppies?

She had to help those kids if she could. They *needed* her.

Spike sounded happy enough, and he was certainly old enough to look out for himself. He could always duck if a stray dart came flying his way.

And she'd speak with Marguerite, of course, as a friend. They could just start talking again. Not about Cree, but about themselves. Like in the old days.

Marguerite never had to find out that her old friend was the listener, Quinney thought, crossing her fingers for luck.

She chewed her lower lip and stared up at the sky. Who did she want to be, she wondered—the big expert on other people's lives, always giving advice, or just an ordinary kid?

Quinney wished there was someone *she* could ask.

Chapter Eighteen

If It Weren't for You

Brynn stretched out her plump sunburned legs and inspected them. "If it turns to tan, I'll be okay," she announced. "If it peels, I'll be the only person in Lake Geneva wearing sweatpants for the rest of the summer."

"How did you get so burned, anyway?" Quinney asked. She had just finished lunch when Brynnie called, suggesting that they meet at Papa's. Quinney watched her friend take a lick of strawberry ice cream.

"Well, I was helping my mom with this new cleaning job on Saturday after I talked to you," Brynn began. "You remember—when I was on my bike. Anyway, we were working for that guy you told us about."

She must mean Sam! "Oh yeah," Quinney said, trying to look casual.

"So we went over there, and you should have *seen* this place."

"Really a mess, huh?" Quinney asked.

"I guess, but it's gorgeous. Right on the river, Quinney. And this great house that just sort of rambles. It's big!" Brynn's cramped little house—a mobile home that hadn't gone anywhere in years—seemed to get smaller every year.

"I guess it must have been hard to clean such a big house," Quinney suggested, sympathetic.

"We made a start, anyway. We're going back later this week. He said to go ahead and throw out all these old newspapers and magazines, just don't tell him about it. He's funny! So I bundled some stuff up for recycling and dumped the rest. Mom started in on the living room and the dining room, then she hit the kitchen. He even asked her to cook dinner—he paid extra. See, he's trying to impress his girlfriend." Brynn looked a little sad when she said this.

"Well, what's wrong with that?" Quinney asked.

Brynn lowered her voice, although there was no one else around. "I think my mom kind of likes him," she confided.

Quinney was flabbergasted. *Sam?* "Your mom likes him? But she barely even knows him."

"Well, see, that's the thing! He was there the whole time we were cleaning, and partway through, he told us to take a break. We ended up taking a long one, and he even paid us for the break time."

"That was nice of him," Quinney said.

"He's a nice guy," Brynn said. "Kind of a slob, but nice. So I decided to go swimming in the river—I went in wearing my shorts and T-shirt. He's got this perfect place for swimming, Quinney, you wouldn't believe it. But that's how I got sunburned, drying off on the grass."

"Did your mom go in the water too?"

"No, she stayed behind on the porch drinking iced tea and talking with Sam."

Uh-oh, Quinney thought. Because Sam was great—until he opened his mouth.

"It was probably the closest she's come to having a date in three years, Quinney," Brynn said, her pink face serious, "ever since she swore off men. Not that it was a real date," she added, frowning. "I mean, from his point of view, he was just talking with his cleaning lady while he was getting ready to impress his girlfriend that night."

"His ex-girlfriend," Quinney corrected her.

Uh-oh.

"What makes you think that?" Brynn asked.

"I don't know—I was just guessing," Quinney gabbled, hoping desperately that Brynnie wouldn't realize what had just happened.

"Anyway," Brynn continued, sighing, "at least my

mom finally had some fun, and she made good money, too. She says thanks for the business, by the way."

"And your mom really liked talking to this guy?" Quinney couldn't resist asking, still not able to believe it.

"Oh, yeah. She said it's generally hard to find such a good conversationalist nowadays, to find a man who can really *listen*, like Sam." Brynn sighed. "It's too bad about the girlfriend. Poor Mom."

Sam was waiting for Quinney at the library, bright-eyed and alert, when she walked in the door. He looked like a big happy squirrel, Quinney thought. "You're early," she said, startled. It was only four thirty-five.

"I couldn't wait, Quincy," he exclaimed. "I just *have* to tell you what happened!"

Mrs. Arbuckle was busying herself with returned books behind the front desk, but Quinney could tell she was listening. She couldn't help it, really—Quinney and Sam were standing right in front of her. "Let's go sit down," Quinney told Sam.

They walked back to the reference room and scooted their heavy oak chairs in close to the table. Quinney looked a little sadly around the familiar room, remembering the excitement of all her meetings.

Was it really almost over?

And what would she do next?

"Well, first of all," Sam was saying, "I want to thank you for what you told me last week. About listening."

"That's okay," Quinney mumbled. "Anyway, *I* was the one who was supposed to be doing the listening."

Sam ignored her last comment. "And thanks for telling me to stop being such a slob and to clean up my house," he continued.

"I don't think that's exactly what I—"

"Because you were right," he said firmly. "I could see the difference right away after Agnes and her daughter got started."

"Agnes?" For just a second, Quinney forgot the name of Brynnie's mom.

"That cleaning lady you recommended," he said, his voice softening. "She came over on Saturday and brought her little girl. A real doll," he added, "to help her mama like that."

"I know the daughter," Quinney said. "She's one of my best friends." *Little girl,* she thought, disgusted.

"That's nice, Quincy. She's a sweetheart, and so is her mother."

"And she cooked dinner for you and—and Cynthia?"

"Cynthia? Oh, yeah," he said dismissively. "Yeah, Agnes made this casserole like you wouldn't believe. It was a *dream* casserole. And you should have seen the old place, Quincy—well, the living room, dining room, and kitchen, anyway—it was perfect. All mopped down, dusted, vacuumed. Windows sparkling, daylilies everywhere. Table all set, candles. And this great smell floating out of the kitchen. *Dinner,*" he said reverently.

"So Cynthia liked it?"

"Liked it? Well, no, as a matter of fact, she hated it. Cracked me up!" Sam chortled. "She accused me of having a new girlfriend," he said. "She told me she could tell by the way things looked! Said I'd invited her over for dinner just to throw it in her face. The new girlfriend, not the dinner."

"But—but didn't you explain?"

Sam shrugged and smiled. "Why bother? I was listening to her shriek away, and I thought, 'Who needs this?' So I just nodded. Apologized, even, just to get rid of her. She left early."

"She did?" Quinney asked, confused. All that work for nothing, and Sam didn't even sound sad!

Sam nodded again. "It was a good thing, too—gave me time to think. And you know what I came up with?"

By now, Quinney figured she could never guess, not in a hundred years.

Because what did she know about people?

Nothing. Zip. "No," she said. "What?"

"Agnes," he announced, triumphant.

"Agnes? You mean Brynnie's mom?"

"That's right. We got to talking that day. Really *talking*, I mean—the two of us! She has a lot to say for herself. She's a very intelligent woman, did you know that, Quincy?"

"I've never talked with her much," Quinney admitted. "I do know she's very nice, though."

"She's had it pretty rough, she and that little girl of hers. Not that she was complaining at all—I just read between the lines," Sam said proudly. "I listened!"

"I know that Brynn and her mom have had some bad luck," Quinney said.

"Well, maybe all that's about to change," Sam said, sounding thoughtful. "They're coming over again tomorrow to start in on the rest of the house. I'm going to see if I can't get them to stay to dinner. With me cooking, this time. I'm a pretty good cook," he added shyly. "You think I have a chance with Agnes?"

"I don't have the slightest idea," Quinney barely managed to say.

Sam looked at her, dismayed.

"No, wait!" Quinney said, collecting herself. "I'd say it's a definite maybe with Mrs. Mathers. Good luck, Sam," she added, smiling.

"I owe it all to you, Quincy," Sam said. He sounded grateful.

"No, you don't," Quinney said flatly. "I was mainly trying to help you win back Cynthia. I didn't know you were going to fall for Brynn's mom."

"But none of it would have happened if it weren't for you," Sam insisted. "Anyway, I wasn't talking about that. I was talking about what you told me about conversation. Remember? You told me to shut up and listen. And I did."

Shut up and listen, Quinney thought, staring out the library window. Sam had left early, too full of his plans to sit still any longer.

Hey, she thought—I should write a how-to book, and call it that. It could be her new career! Her old one was certainly not working out the way she'd intended. How could she have been so wrong about Sam? She had thought he was hopeless.

Quinney sighed and stared down at the dollar bill Sam had given her for his final listening appointment.

Nothing had gone the way she'd planned, she thought. Look at Toby—poor, lonely Toby. All he had wanted in this whole wide world was someone to play with, and she wouldn't even introduce him to the twins. *No, they wouldn't like each other,* she mimicked herself.

Hah! She'd only been trying to keep her own secret, she admitted now—she hadn't really been thinking of Toby at all.

Lucky for Toby that his mom had interrupted his schedule long enough to take him out for a walk, Quinney thought. Hey, maybe she should write a how-to book for moms! She could call it *Stop Pestering Your Kid*.

Quinney busied herself folding the dollar up smaller and smaller, thinking about Ms. Ryder and Spike. What about *them*? Spike had started out blaming her, Quinney, for the fact that his wife was never home. She should write another book and call it *Blame Me! No-Fault Marriage*.

But why stop there? Quinney winced, thinking of Cree—and of Marguerite. Wow, she could write a book for girls called *How To Lose Your First Boyfriend Before You Even Have One*.

"So," a harsh voice said. Quinney jumped a little in her library chair, and the folded dollar bill bounced out of her hands onto the table.

"Here, add this to your scuzzy little pile of cash— I was about to mail it to you." Another dollar seemed to float down out of the air. Quinney looked up.

It was Cree.

"What—what—what—"

"What am I *doing* here?" he finished the sentence for her, his voice cool. He swung a long leg over the chair opposite Quinney—Sam's chair—like he was climbing onto a horse, and he sat down. "It's a free country, right?" he asked, sounding sarcastic. "I was here in the library. And gee, I heard this familiar voice giving advice." He peered around the small reference room in an exaggerated way. "Well, where are your friends?" he asked.

"My—my—they're not here," Quinney said, trying to pull herself together. "Why *would* they be?"

Cree shrugged. "That's the joke, isn't it?" he asked. "To laugh at all the jerks like me who write to you for help?" His expression was stony, almost calm, but his eyes glittered with anger.

"Cree, no!" Quinney said.

"So you *do* know my name," he said triumphantly. "And it was you at the bowling alley, of course."

"Well, yes," Quinney admitted, "but nobody's laughing at you. No one knows that I'm doing this, I swear! It was all my own brilliant idea," she added bitterly.

"I don't believe you," Cree said. "This has got to be a joke."

"Well, it's not," Quinney said. "*I'm* the joke. I thought the listening business would be easy—you know, how hard could it be? I'm used to being the one with the answers. *Little Miss Know-It-All*," she said, repeating Marguerite's hurtful words. "That's me."

"Wait a minute—let me get this straight," Cree said, holding up one hand. "This whole thing was your idea, and you didn't tell anyone else about it? No one at all?"

Quinney nodded her head, miserable. She willed herself not to cry.

"And you took out the ad in the paper by yourself, and everything?" Cree continued, relentless.

Quinney nodded again.

"But why?" Cree asked, bewildered. "Was it for the money? For kicks? *Why*?" he repeated. He leaned forward, waiting for her reply.

"Not for kicks, I promise," Quinney said. "Believe me, it wasn't that much fun. Maybe it was for the money, a little bit. But it was mostly—oh, I don't know how to explain it."

"Try," he said, the corner of his mouth turning up in what was almost a smile.

Could it be a smile?

Quinney took a deep breath. "Well, I—"

"Excuse me," a soft voice interrupted. It was the librarian, Mrs. Arbuckle! Quinney had never been so happy to see her. "The library closed a few minutes ago. I didn't hear you two—you're so quiet back here. I'm glad I didn't lock you in," she added.

Locked in the library with Cree Scovall! Quinney blushed just thinking about it. She jumped to her feet, and Cree slowly pushed back his chair and stood up.

"Is that your money on the table, young man?" Mrs. Arbuckle asked Cree. "Don't forget it, now."

"It's hers," Cree said, nodding at Quinney. "She earned it."

Quinney scooped up the dollar bills, stuffed them into her pocket, and headed for the entrance to the library. "Well, bye," she called blindly over her shoulder. Escape was in sight!

"Wait—I'll walk you home," Cree said coolly.

"No, that's okay. You really don't have to walk with me," Quinney said to Cree under her breath.

She couldn't believe it. Here she was, Quinney Todd, trying to talk *Cree Scovall* out of walking her home!

"Oh yes I do," Cree said, keeping his voice low. "We're not finished yet."

Chapter Nineteen ☎ **Real Friends**

Quinney and Cree walked down the library path and then hesitated when they reached the sidewalk. "Which way?" Cree finally asked.

"Huh?"

"Do we go left or right?" he asked again. "Where do you live? And what's your name, by the way?"

"It's Quinney, Quinney Todd. And we have to go left, then cut back toward the lake," she said.

She wished that she had decided to wear her new T-shirt for her meeting with Sam, instead of the faded navy one she had on.

"Come on, then, *Quinney*, let's start walking," Cree said, sounding a little impatient.

Quinney tried to secretly glance around her as she walked, hoping no one she knew would see her with Cree. Especially not Marguerite.

On the other hand, though, she wished a photographer would leap out of the bushes and capture this incredible moment on film—for her to keep for all eternity! Even if Cree *was* still furious with her, which he seemed to be.

"So, start talking," Cree said, after a few moments. "You were about to explain why you wanted to be a professional listener."

"Well, for one thing, I figured it was something I was already good at," Quinney began. "Listening, I mean. I'm pretty quiet. Actually," she confided, "it's hard to get a word in edgewise at my house sometimes. It can be kind of a zoo." They turned the corner and headed toward the lake.

Quinney tried to walk as slowly as she could.

"Tell me about it," Cree said with a laugh that sounded more like a bark. "Same at my house."

Quinney peeked at him through her long bangs. He didn't look as angry as he had before, she noticed with relief. "But the thing was," she continued, "people expected advice, too. Listening wasn't good enough."

"You do give pretty good advice," Cree admitted.

"Thanks, but if I did, it was by accident," Quinney said, making a face.

"And what's another thing?" Cree asked, after they'd walked in silence for a while.

"What do you mean?"

Cree shrugged. "You said you were good at the

listening business, for one thing. So what was another reason you did it?"

Cree was a listener too, Quinney realized. Too careful a listener, maybe. "Well," she admitted slowly, "I guess the job made me feel smart."

"Why?" Cree asked. "Because the people who wrote you needed help, but you didn't? You felt smarter than them? *Better* than them?"

"Maybe a little, at first," Quinney admitted. "But I never thought that the people who wrote to me were really dumb or anything. I just mean it made me feel good to be the one answering questions. I guess it made me feel like my life must really be okay if I could do that."

"But it's not," Cree stated, as if this were a known fact—or at least a familiar idea. "So what's wrong with your life?"

"Nothing, really!" Quinney protested. "I mean, compared to other people's lives, where *real* stuff is wrong. It's just that my two best friends don't really like each other anymore, and there's nothing I can do about it. And—and I don't feel like I belong, sometimes—in my family, I mean," she confided in a rush. "It's like I'm just floating around somewhere. My mom even said that to me once. It's kind of like I've been taking care of all of them lately in a way, and I don't know why."

"Do your parents make you do it?" Cree asked.

"No," Quinney admitted, her words tumbling out. "Not really. I guess I take care of them for the same reasons I started listening, because I'm good at it and because it makes me feel smart. It makes me feel *real*," she added, surprising herself.

"But you're just what, thirteen?" Cree asked, tilting his head as he looked at her.

"Yeah, thirteen," Quinney fibbed. Well, if Cree could lie about his age, so could she.

Cree shook his head. "But shouldn't you be doing kid stuff, instead of grown-up stuff like trying to solve everyone's problems?"

Kid stuff—what an insult!

But it was weird, Quinney thought suddenly. Cree kind of reminded her of herself, giving similar advice to Mrs. Toby. "I'm not a little kid," she objected, slowing her pace even more. She was almost home, but she didn't want this conversation to end. Ever.

"Oh, come on," Cree scoffed. "I didn't mean teeter-totters and swings. I just meant—you know, having fun. Hanging out. Talking. Making new friends."

The part about making friends sounded pretty good, Quinney thought, stealing another look at Cree. Then she sighed, thinking of Marguerite—who had what was practically a date with Cree that very night.

Would her old friend always be three steps ahead of her?

And what would Marguerite say if she could see Quinney right now?

"So what about it?" Cree was asking.

"I'm sorry—what about what?" Quinney stopped walking.

She was home.

"Well, I was *trying* to say that we could meet at the library sometimes, and just talk. For *free*," Cree emphasized, sounding stern. "You know, you say something dumb, and then I say something dumb, and nobody's an expert. You're kind of gutsy," he added approvingly. "I want to hear what crazy thing you come up with next—even if you mess up, Little Miss Know-It-All. Besides," he added, grinning, "you can tell me more about Marguerite."

"Okay," Quinney said, almost overcome by a mind-boggling mixture of elation, shyness, and gloom. She stared down at the familiar sidewalk in front of her house as if seeing it for the first time. "Um—do you want your dollar back?"

Cree threw back his head and laughed. "No," he said finally, "you keep it. Like I told that librarian, you earned it fair and square."

Chapter Twenty

The Funniest Thing

The old white house was quiet as she opened the front door. Quinney paused in the hallway, listening to its familiar creaks. Smudge marks Teddy-and-Mack-high decorated the painted doorframe.

The living room door was partially closed; Quinney could hear the murmur of voices. "This time I get to be Peter Pan," Mack was saying. "*I* get to fly."

"Okay," Teddy said, "but fly quiet, or else Mom will come in and wreck everything."

"And let's say I get to be Captain Hook, okay?" a third voice said.

It was Toby!

Oh yeah, Quinney remembered. The famous sleepover was tonight.

She might have some explaining to do soon, she thought, unless she could get to Toby first. She'd ask him privately to keep their secret. He was a great

192

kid—he wouldn't blab. *Maybe.*

Quinney grinned, thinking of how surprised her little friend would be to see her again.

No, she corrected herself—Toby was the *twins'* friend now.

"Let's say I'm the crocodile this time," Teddy was saying. He started to *tick-tock* loudly.

"But what about Monty?" Toby asked. "What'll he be?"

"He's Smee," Mack said, raising his voice above his brother's clock noises. "He's *always* Smee."

"Oh, cool," Toby said. "Avast!"

Quinney turned and walked through the dining room—her mother's studio—toward the kitchen. Over the scent of turpentine and oil paints, something smelled good. Dinner must be almost ready. It was tuna casserole, she could tell—a family favorite.

As she started to push open the swinging door that led into the kitchen, she heard her parents' voices, low and cozy. They were sitting at the kitchen table, talking. Quinney hesitated. "But what would be fun for the whole family to do?" her father was asking.

"Not hiking," Mrs. Todd said emphatically. "Monty always complains."

"And we agreed bowling is out, until the twins are a couple of years older," Mr. Todd said. "So that leaves—what?"

"You know," Quinney's mother said slowly, "I heard the funniest thing when I was at the market this afternoon, and it's given me a crazy idea."

"Let's hear it," her husband said. Quinney could almost picture the eager expression on his face.

"Well," Mrs. Todd began, "apparently there's an ad in the *Save-a-Cent* that has everyone talking. There's this 'professional listener' in town, it seems, and it only costs a dollar for a fifteen-minute appointment."

Quinney thought her heart was going to stop beating.

"Who is it, do you know?" Mr. Todd said, laughing.

"No, but who cares? The price is right, and it sounds like fun! What if I write in and ask for an appointment? Maybe this listener can give us a few ideas. Give us some answers."

No, no, don't do it, Quinney thought, trying hard to send her brain waves through the door and into the kitchen. *I don't have answers anymore, I have questions!*

She had questions.

Such a thought made her feel strange—but I'll just have to get used to that, Quinney thought. Little by little does the trick.

"Go for it," Mr. Todd was urging his wife. "It couldn't hurt, and maybe the professional listener will come up with something we can do together. You know, as a family."

"Do you dare me?" his wife asked, teasing.

"I double dare you!"

"Okay—I'm going to go get a postcard right now," Mrs. Todd said. "You can help me write it."

Quinney heard a chair squeak as it was pushed away from the table.

She took a deep breath, straightened her shoulders, and stepped into the warm kitchen.

It was time to talk.